Valentine

by

Sara Guzman

Valentine is a work of fiction. The characters and events in this book are fictitious. Any similarity to real persons, living or dead, is coincidental and not intended by the author.

ISBN-13: 978-957-43-4746-9

First edition: July 2017

10 9 8 7 6 5 4 3 2 1

The cover shows a detail from
Ferdinand Hodler's "Night" (1890)

VALENTINE

for Jane

SARA GUZMAN

CONTENTS

SARA GUZMAN

PROLOGUE

When Christine was twelve years old, she did that thing with the full moon and the bowl of water and the razor blade. She intoned the incantation – the one that ends with "let me see my love tonight" – touched the razor to her lips, kissed it, and stared at the hypnotic surface of the water.

She doesn't remember going to sleep that night, but the next morning she woke up in her bed as usual. She'd seen – or said she'd seen, or thought she'd seen, or at least she told all her friends that she'd seen – the stubbled sun-bronzed unsmiling face, almost gaunt but definitely handsome, of a man who, ten years older than her, newlywed and over a thousand miles away, was at that very moment deflowering his first bride.

A man who, as she said, was to die for.

CHAPTER 1

Cancun – August 27, 2003

Luiz was driving pretty well, all things considered. Of course, he drove like an entitled prick at the best of times. It was one of the few things that Christine didn't like about him. At least, it used to be only a few things. These days it seemed like there were more and more.

She turned around to check how Emma and Benito were doing in the back seat. As usual, Luiz had left the top down, and the air was really blowing around back there. The wind and Benito's hands had gotten well inside Emma's summer-thin party dress. By the treacherous light of the moon, their fused faces seemed to run together, and amid their flying hair and loose flapping clothes, all that Christine could really make out was a vague expressionist image of hot, fluid passion.

She turned to Luiz. She saw the cuts on his hands, the speckles of blood – another man's blood – still on his cheek. Maybe the left-over adrenaline from the fight was somehow countering the effects of all the coke and alcohol. Or maybe it was just the sobering rush of warm night air, but even though he was sitting right next to her, he seemed impossibly distant. Who knew where he was really?

He was on his own, separate from her, from the road,

from the ridiculously expensive imported Mercedes he was driving. And everything was an adversary. Even Mexico itself.

Luiz always said that he hated his native land. He told people he was American, and as a good American, he loved American cars. Not those gutless hunks of generic metal that Detroit somehow still managed to dump onto the market, but real American cars, like Mercedes, Lexus and Porsche.

Christine would have found that pretty funny, except that Luiz was serious. She wasn't sure how she felt about that one. She guessed she would have preferred her lover to have a sense of humor, but on the other hand, she found his naivete strangely endearing.

Even his sense of entitlement had its up side. When he tore past a lurking cop car and it pulled out behind them with its lights flashing and siren blaring, she knew there was no way in hell he was ever going to pull over – and if you had any romance in your soul, how could you fail to admire him for that? She knew it put them all in danger – because now Luiz's recklessness was going to go all the way to eleven – but outside of death or terrible injury, she also knew that whatever happened, at least they weren't going to get into trouble. Trouble didn't come from the cops. Trouble was what happened when you went to the club.

And one thing about Luiz was that he loved to dance.

Which was why, earlier that evening, Luiz and Benito had swung by the beachside villa outside Tulum. They'd picked up Christine and Emma, and the four of them had blasted up the highway to Cancun. In the open-top luxury car, with the inky-black moonlit Caribbean flashing past on their right and the sweet-smelling night flowers in the patches of jungle on their left, sitting next to a hot guy who was rich, powerful, dangerous, and wearing just the right amount of bling, it was easy for Christine to tell herself she had it made. The drugs that were coursing through her blood didn't hurt either.

Luiz was no elitist. He preferred the down-market clubs that catered to tourists. It might have been that he liked to show off and figured that he made a bigger splash with the Nortenos, or it might have been, like he said, that the tourist night-clubs played better music. By which he meant music that was more authentically 'American'.

In any case, whichever club he chose on any given night, they didn't need to worry about standing in line. Luiz pulled up right outside the entrance and tossed the keys to the valet – Christine had never actually seen him give anything to anyone; he took from the hands of others, whether they were willing or not, but he never put anything into another's hand – as they jumped or clambered out.

Once inside, he allowed himself to be recognized by inferiors and equals, and after some discrete pharmaceutical refueling in the section, they hit the dance floor.

For Christine, this was the real high. The beats washed over her mind, and the pulsing music inhabited her lithe, sun-tanned body, so that her breasts and hips strained to escape from the fabric of her dress. A faint, beguiling, Mona Lisa smile of deep rapture suffused her face. She knew who she was. She knew where she was. She was deliriously at peace, and she was one with the surging crowd.

She danced with Luiz some of the time, but mostly he left her for women who were better dancers. She didn't mind. He was a fantastic partner, and she liked dancing with him, but she knew she wasn't in his league. She was grateful to escape the pressure.

Luiz on the other hand could be jealous, and Christine found it was impossible to know what would set him off. She could be grinding away, provocative as any hooker, drifting from one guy to another all night, and Luiz didn't turn a hair. But somehow all of these casual partners knew that there was a line they weren't allowed to cross. And they knew instinctively what would happen if they did.

But some men weren't in on the code. Bobby for instance. She didn't know his real name, but that was how she thought of him. An American college kid, hot and smooth as the Devil, down on the Mexican Riviera for a long weekend of sun and sex. High on the usual cocktail of party drugs, he went beyond the harmless formalities of flirting. He was hitting on Christine for real, and had no idea that he was trying to punch way above his weight.

Luiz attacked him without warning, coming in from the side. Two fast jabs, low and vicious. Christine's scream was lost beneath the thudding music, but the crowd shrunk away in a moment, like a jellyfish sprayed with acid, and Bobby took advantage of the suddenly empty space to reel away from Luiz and catch his breath.

A knife appeared in Bobby's hand. Christine wondered how he'd got it past the bouncers. She realized that Bobby the kid was maybe not so wet behind the ears after all.

Luiz grinned and produced a bottle.

"Luiz, no!"

Luiz raised his free hand toward her with the index finger extended in warning. Christine didn't dare say anything more – and what was there she could say anyway? It was all up to Bobby now. She hoped he'd have the sense to run.

The music and lights hadn't missed a beat, but you could feel the bouncers pushing their way through the churning mass of people, caught in a desperate nightmarish run through treacle to shut this thing down before it began.

But then Benito stepped into the circle, and Bobby spooked. He lunged at Luiz, who dodged away with a dancer's grace and elegantly clubbed the side of Bobby's head. Bobby's knees gave out, and Luiz and Benito were on him like wolves, punching and kicking him to the ground.

The crowd devoured the show like it was reality TV,

pretending to hide their eyes while they stole furtive glances and shared shouted whispers.

It was all over in moments. Five or six bouncers waded out from the crowd and grabbed Luiz and Benito from behind. They were careful not to mess with them any more than they had to, and Luiz and Benito offered no resistance. Adrenaline and victory is a heady mix. Somehow Luiz must have punched Bobby's knife because his hand was bleeding. But that was nothing. Honor was satisfied, and Luiz was pleased, for the moment, to be magnanimous. Benito followed his lead.

The bouncers would have shrugged if their over-muscled shoulders would have let them. They just figured that the deed was done. And now that the easy part was over, they had to deal with the mess: peeling Bobby off the dance floor, and getting Luiz and Benito to leave the club without pissing them off.

As the four of them were ushered outside, Christine thought to herself: I did that. She felt a confused mix of emotions. She knew it wasn't her fault – she hadn't wanted Bobby to get beaten up, and she hoped that he was OK – but when she looked deep inside herself, she also discovered that she wasn't sorry.

She thought about that again now, with the chemical high and the lights of Cancun receding behind them, while the lights of the wailing cop car came steadily closer. She wondered what she'd become.

Luiz sped along the highway. It was unlit, but mostly straight and well paved, and so far he hadn't tried any fancy maneuvers.

In the back seat, Emma huddled and giggled, thrilled by the novelty of the chase. For her it was a new emotional experience, like something out of the movies. Benito took it in stride. For him too it was a form of entertainment, and he amused Emma by looking behind them and feeding her an imaginative running commentary on their pursuers.

Christine realized that although Luiz had no intention of stopping, he also wasn't putting any real effort into getting away. If he'd wanted to outrun the cops, the Mercedes could have left their underpowered vehicle in the dust – which might have led to a roadblock up ahead where anything could have happened, but she knew Luiz wasn't the kind of guy to make decisions out of prudence.

So when the cop car moved into the fast lane and drew alongside them at one hundred fifty kilometers per hour, it was only because Luiz had cold-bloodedly decided to let them.

The cop in the passenger seat turned a flashlight on Luiz. Luiz grinned at him and waved a greeting like he was under a spotlight.

Christine saw the cops' mouths move in urgent conversation.

She also saw the red tail-lights of another vehicle noodling along in the slow lane half a mile ahead.

Then Luiz did something Christine had hardly ever seen him do before. He used his turn signal, expressing his clear intention to change lanes and overtake.

The cop driver probably intended to drop back, because when Luiz barged into them, the Mercedes was already half a car length ahead, so that Luiz's door struck their front fender.

It was kind of hard to see what happened after that. But in the rear-view – for some reason, Christine didn't even think about turning around – the cop car spun out and left the road in a cloud of dust. There didn't seem to be any flames, so that was good. Christine also hoped it hadn't rolled. Rolling was bad news, even in a cop car.

Meanwhile, the Mercedes just rocked slightly and flew on as though nothing had happened. Benito whooped and went apeshit, pumping his fist and grasping Luiz's hand. Emma sat with her mouth open, making Christine wonder what she'd expected or if she was just in shock. Christine also ransacked her short-term memory and tried to figure out if she'd actually physically felt any impact or not.

CHAPTER 2

Next day at the villa, Christine woke some time in the early afternoon. Her mouth was as dry as the dead potted plant she'd dragged in from the terrace earlier that summer to protect it from a hurricane that was supposed to make landfall fifty miles to the north. The hurricane never came, and she'd never gotten around to dragging the plant back outside again.

Last night, after they'd rolled back home, vacuumed up a few more lines and downed a few more shots, Luiz had made love to her as passionately as he had all those months ago when she first agreed to go to bed with him.

He was, as they say, a considerate lover. And as a dancer, he was skilled and surprisingly graceful too. And the man had the constitution of an ox. Or no, nothing so clichéd and brutish. Maybe a pinata. But that wasn't right either. You could hit Luiz with anything and he'd never fall apart. He was indestructible. A force of nature, strong and full of terrible passion, but indifferent to your feelings – and to the destruction he wrought. He was like a hurricane. Like the hurricane that had never come.

And now the other half of her wrecked bed was empty. As she'd expected, Luiz had already left. She wondered if he'd even stayed with her through the rest of the night.

She also wondered if he'd ever come back. And if he did,

whether he'd ever make love to her again. She had no illusions about her place in Luiz's world. The villa belonged to him, and although nothing had ever been said out loud, they both understood that he owned her as much as he owned the villa.

This was her gilded cage and she was his whore, his pet Yanqui.

But then again, where was the harm? They were both old enough to know what they were doing. Of course it wasn't going to last forever – he could turn her out at any time for any reason – but right now they were both having a blast. There was nothing sordid about it. She thought of herself as a courtesan, and the role appealed to her.

The chink of crockery brought Christine back to full consciousness. Emma was moving stuff around in the kitchen. Christine got off the bed, threw on a wrap and padded out to see what was up.

"Hey. Are you making coffee?"

"Just drip."

"Good enough."

"And there's juice. And fruit. And flat champagne."

"Jesus, we did champagne too? I don't even remember. But I guess that would explain a lot."

"Yeah, it was definitely the champagne."

"We should tell them we're not going to be drinking any more of that expensive shit again."

"We should totally do that. A girl has to have standards."

Christine pulled opened the fridge and rummaged around inside.

"We don't have any milk?"

She put coffee, juice, a bowl of cereal and a pineapple on the kitchen table. She sat down and poured coconut milk on the cereal.

"Benito still here?"

"He was but he got a call. I think from Luiz. Hey, that

was some crazy shit last night."

Christine didn't answer right away. Then –

"You think those cops were OK?"

"You see their faces when they saw it was Luiz? That was kind of scary, you know? I mean, to you and me, he's just Luiz, but to those guys, he's like a seriously big deal. Benito too."

"It's nothing we didn't already know".

"Knowing it and seeing it aren't the same. And what about that guy he beat up?"

"I wish he hadn't done that."

"It was just for dancing with you, right? And 'Nito said he had a knife. Hey, what's that on your cereal?"

"This? It's all I could find –"

"Oh hey!" Emma fished a half-smoked joint out of her shorts pocket. "You want me to spark this up, or should I go find us some rum?"

Later that same afternoon, Christine was swimming alone in the sea. She loved the feel of the salt water on her skin, the way it macerated her flesh and polished her like a pebble when she dove beneath the waves. She thought she heard Emma's shouts even from underwater, and sure enough when she broke the surface with her shoulder-length brown hair flat and glistening against the contours of her head and neck, there was Emma pacing anxiously on the sand.

Emma wasn't so keen on the physical aspects of living near the beach, even when it was a beach as perfect as this one. The granite-topped counter in her en-suite bathroom was cluttered with restorative formulas and protective potions to save her hair and fair skin from the ravages of sun and salt. Standing on the yellow-white sand with the fringe of green and gray coconut palms behind her, she looked two-dimensional, like a page out of a fashion magazine. Her naturally wavy auburn hair was tied up in a scarf and she was wearing lip gloss.

"Christine, stop fucking around. You need to get back to the house."

Christine waded out of the surf.

"What's going on?"

"Luiz is back. He wants to talk to you. And keep away from me with all that salt water will you?"

Christine playfully flicked her hand and splashed her with a few inconsequential droplets. But Emma was in no mood – "Jesus, you're such a child" – and she petulantly stalked away without waiting for Christine to pick up her towel.

Luiz had made himself at home in the living room, spreading himself out on the soft white leather of the Italian sofa. He looked relaxed, like he had all the time in the world, and Christine immediately sensed danger.

"You don't even get dressed for me?"

Christine was still in her two-piece swimsuit. It wasn't the sort of outfit that Luiz would normally have objected to.

"I'm sorry. I came straight from the beach when Emma told me you were here."

She hadn't even taken a shower. She could feel the prickle of the tiny crystals of salt on her skin.

"I need you to do something for me."

"What is it?"

"'What is it?' You don't say this to me. You say, 'sure'."

"Sure, Luiz, you know I will. Whatever you want."

Luiz stood up. He crossed the room to speak to her up close, face to face.

"It's about last night. Word has come down. 'It's your bitches, Luiz. They do nothing, and when you're with them you cause too much trouble.' No, you don't say nothing. I tell you when to speak. This is what they say."

Christine kept a respectful silence. She didn't know if she was supposed to respond or not, but in any case she had no idea what he wanted her to say.

"Instead of you do nothing, this is what you do, yes? You drive north, to America, you meet a man, and then you come back to me again."

"When?"

She'd meant to say — to scream at him until he went away — No! I can't do it! I know how this ends and I won't. There's just no fucking way! But somehow it had come out as "when?"

"Tonight. Here is your American passport. And I packed some of your things."

He gave Christine her passport and snapped his fingers. Emma came in with an overnight bag full of Christine's clothes.

"Luiz, I know I owe you, but this? I don't think I can."

It was as much as she dared say. Luiz took her chin in his hand.

"Listen to me. You can because you must. You must do this thing for me or it will all be over. Everything. Do you understand?"

Christine looked into his eyes and saw nothing. His hand was still gripping her jaw. She nodded.

"It has to be tonight?"

The light airplane droned steadily northward through the night sky. Christine had no idea what kind it was, but from the inside it looked incredibly flimsy, like a clown car with wings that might detach at any moment. It felt more like a toy than a machine that could actually carry people through the air.

Below them, the empty land was a slowly turning darkness, but above and all around, she was surprised to see so much activity. They seemed to be swimming through a soup of other aircraft, each one intent upon its own mysterious purpose. Even stranger, these other aircraft were all invisible, their existence inferred only from a shifting configuration of running lights and colored navigation beacons that wheeled in unison across the sky.

They'd taken off soon after sunset from a private airstrip outside Tulum. For some reason, she'd thought that Luiz might fly with her, but he didn't even drive her out to the plane. Instead he'd sent Benito to pick her up from the villa, which made for an uncomfortable ride. Neither of them spoke. Christine had always liked 'Nito, but they both felt the weight of Emma's lurking presence. And anyway, Christine belonged of course to Luiz, so nothing was ever going to happen. They both resented these unspoken constraints, and when they were together, they both experienced vague feelings of anger. It made them awkward with each other.

So even as they drove away from the villa, Christine already felt the ground shifting beneath her. She realized that nothing was going to play out as she expected. She was off balance from the start.

At the airfield, Benito delivered her to a man she'd never met before. This man led her out onto the tarmac and introduced her to the pilot, who was sitting at the controls of his idling airplane. The pilot nodded to her and indicated that she should fasten her seat harness.

And now the plane seemed to be descending. Were they coming in to land? Christine had no very clear idea of what she was supposed to do. Luiz had mentioned driving, but here she was in an airplane. Had he misspoken? When they landed, would she still be in Mexico or would she already be across the border? Perhaps Luiz had simply stashed the drugs – it had to be drugs – along with her clothes in the overnight bag.

She twisted around and stared at the bag, which had been strapped into the seat behind them. Was she allowed to open it? Did she even want to?

For a moment, she was overcome with a wave of help-lessness and self-pity. She had no idea where she was and no control over where she was being taken. She wondered what would happen if she attacked the pilot. The doors seemed to open easily enough, so if she caught him by surprise, could she push him out of the plane? She'd have to fly the thing herself, but that didn't faze her. Flying didn't look so hard and she fig-ured she only had to make one successful landing. And when she was back on the ground, she'd be on her own. She could disappear. She'd be free to cross the border for real and head for the Northwest, maybe even go back home...

She gazed out of her window. Off to their right, just below the horizon, the lights of a city polluted the sky.

"Senor?"

The pilot turned to her. She gestured toward the distant glow.

"America?"

"Si, America. Brownsville."

"Is that where we're going?"

He shook his head and pointed at the terrain ahead of them.

"See?"

She made out the lights of a quiet airfield, the unmistak-able layout of a landing strip.

"Is that Mexico? Or is it America?"

The pilot just laughed.

"That is where we land."

Down on the ground they were met by a big black Hum-mer and a late model Dodge sedan that was so nondescript it didn't even seem to be any particular color. The Dodge had Texas plates. They told her it was hers, and that she was to deliver it to an address outside Brownsville before noon that same day. They warned her not to write the address down, and they impressed upon her the importance of not forgetting it. They explained which direction was north and told her the border was about four hours away. She could expect to reach it shortly after sunrise.

And then they were gone. The pilot and his airplane had already disappeared, and she was left alone on the tarmac.

She got behind the wheel of the sedan and adjusted the rear view mirror.

Fuck, she thought. Jesus fucking Christ.

She started the engine, pulled out onto the highway and headed north.

At the Matamoros international border crossing, there was already a chaotic tailback of vehicles waiting to be processed. She pushed her way forward like everyone else, fighting for every inch of space and growing more and more anxious about being late. This went on for nearly two hours. By the time she finally reached the head of the line and was waved forward into an inspection bay, she'd almost forgotten how terrified she was of getting busted.

A female Latino border guard in aviator sunglasses tapped on her window. Christine rolled it down.

"Morning, ma'am. Are you a US citizen?"

She handed over her passport. The guard flicked through it.

"Ms Cooper? What was the purpose of your visit to Mexico?"

"Vacation."

"Uh-huh. You have anyone else traveling with you today?"

"What? No, it's just me."

"Uh-huh. Just sit tight for a moment will you?"

The guard disappeared back behind the tinted glass of her booth.

Just sitting there, waiting for whatever happened next, Christine really started jonesing for a cigarette, but she figured this probably wasn't a good time. Also, she realized she'd forgotten to bring any.

A minute later the guard came back out again.

"OK, Ms Cooper, could you pull over into secondary processing and pop the trunk for me, please?"

Shit, thought Christine – and then she immediately panicked because she wasn't sure if she'd said it out loud. 'But so what if I did?' she thought, or said. 'I mean, it's a reasonable reaction. Do they ever get someone who's pleased about getting pulled for secondary?'

She watched the dog handler lead his beagle around the car until she lost sight of him behind the raised lid of the trunk.

"Ms Cooper, you want to step out of the vehicle for me, please?"

"What's the problem?"

"Just step out of the vehicle, please."

Christine stepped out of the vehicle.

Around the back of the car, she saw the dog handler direct the sniffer dog to the contents of her overnight bag, which apparently someone had put in the trunk. The dog acted interested and excited, but did that mean something or was it just how beagles normally behaved?

"How long have you been out of the country?"

"I don't know exactly. A few months. Since before the start of summer."

"Where did you stay?"

"Around Cancun."

"Most people would have flown."

"I guess."

"But not you?"

"I like driving in Mexico."

Stupid stupid stupid. What a dumbass thing to say. Christine kicked herself as she felt the guard's eyes bore into her from behind the intimidating shades.

"You don't hear that too often. Is this your vehicle?"

"Sure"

"You have the registration?"

Christine got back into the car. She checked the sun visor and found nothing, which made her look like a complete idiot and was almost enough to make her confess everything right there and then.

It all depended on the glovebox – which some asshole had locked. She didn't know you could even do that. She fumbled with the keys and got it open and found the registration and gave it to the guard. The guard read out the name on the document:

"Mr Aguilla?"

"All right, look, I don't wear a ring and I never changed my name, and if you have to know, we've been going through some pretty rough times this year, but I still love him and I came home because it's our third anniversary the day after tomorrow."

Christine had no idea where these lies were coming from. She didn't even know what day it was.

The sniffer dog started barking. It had finished checking the trunk and now it was nosing around under the car. The handler pulled the dog away and produced a flashlight.

"You got something?"

"Yeah –"

There was a long pause.

"Roadkill."

The Latina guard held out the registration documents.

"Welcome back to the US, Ms Cooper. Good luck with

your anniversary."

Christine took the papers without a word. She didn't trust herself to speak. She got behind the wheel and started the car —

"Hold on!"

It was the dog handler. Her trunk was still open. He slammed it closed.

Christine drove away. She turned off at the first exit, pulled over to the side of the road and burst into tears.

The address outside Brownsville was easy enough to find. From the highway, it looked like any other failed dirt farm, but as soon as she drove into it, a number of well-dressed men stepped out from the tumbledown outbuildings. Some of them carried weapons in plain sight, and the rest didn't make any particular effort to conceal the fact that they were armed.

Christine parked up in the middle of the yard. One of the men approached her, opened her door and invited her to get out. She was then directed to another man, while the first man got behind the wheel of the Dodge.

The second man led her to a half-ton pickup and told her to get in. She did as instructed, and as they drove away, she looked back and saw the first man drive the Dodge into the shadowed interior of one of the buildings. Large metal doors slid closed behind it. All of the other men had already disappeared, and once again the yard looked like it had been derelict for a hundred years. A place where nothing ever happened.

Sitting beside yet another man who was taking her who knew where, Christine remembered that her bag was still in the trunk. She wondered if the men would be going through her things. Would they even be interested? Either way she realized she didn't care. She wondered if Luiz would feel the same way, but she was too exhausted to think about it. Mostly she just wanted the whole thing to be over.

The pickup pulled into a truck stop. The driver killed the engine and jumped out. In the sudden, unexpected silence, Christine gazed out at the wide, flat fields that ran to the horizon in every direction. She was in the US. She was free to literally walk away. She could set out across this empty country and just keep walking. She could walk forever and no-one would stop her, because this was America.

The driver came back and led her over to where the big rigs were parked.

"This guy's going south. He'll take you to Cancun. You'll be home in twenty-four hours. Here."

He gave her a paper sack.

"What's this?"

"Food. Sandwiches. And something to drink. You have any money?"

"No."

"Take this."

"Forty bucks?"

"You won't need it, but everyone feels better with money in their pocket."

"Thanks."

"You're welcome. Bon voyage."

He left her and walked back to his pickup.

Bon voyage?! thought Christine. Seriously, what the fuck? She clamped the sack of food between her teeth and used both hands to swing herself up into the big rig's cab.

CHAPTER 3

Christine had been back at the villa for three days when the big argument that had been brewing with Emma finally erupted.

They'd spent the whole summer drifting in and out of each other's rooms and hanging out together all through the long, lazy afternoons down at one of the tourist bars further along the beach – people watching, drinking, flirting with who-ever was behind the bar and comparing notes on the finer points of Luiz's and Benito's love-making. But since the drug run to Brownsville, they'd hardly spoken, and Christine was spending more of her time alone, either swimming in the ridiculously blue sea or else dozing in the shade of the palm trees on their private section of beach.

There had been no word from Luiz or Benito either, and that made both of them antsy.

The easy friendship of the two women had soured into a minefield of grievances, and when Christine came wandering back to the villa after an early morning swim, the beach-wrap she was wearing set everything off.

"Who said you could wear that?"

"I didn't think you'd mind. You said I could borrow your stuff."

"Not that one."

"You were asleep, or else I would have asked."

"What, so taking it when I'm unconscious makes it OK? 'Nito gave me that, as if you didn't know."

"Jesus, Emma, it's not like I'm stealing it."

"Then take it off. Right now."

"What the hell's wrong with you?"

"Just do it."

"I'm taking a shower first. You can have it after that. I'll even wash it and put it right back where I found it. It'll be like no-one ever touched it."

"No. Because it's mine. Which means you don't get to decide what happens to it. You might have been queen for a day up in Brownsville, but you're back here now and that day is over, bitch."

"You think Brownsville was such a fucking trip, then next time you can tell Luiz you want to go there yourself. Because here," – she tore off the wrap and threw it to the ground – "you can have my fucking job. I quit. You can have all of it."

Christine stormed out of the room. Emma followed her to the foot of the stairs and called after her –

"I don't want your job, puta, and I don't want your man. Just stay the fuck away from me and 'Nito."

Somewhere upstairs, a door slammed.

It felt strange to be wearing clothes that covered so much of her body. Christine's legs had been bare since the first days of summer, but the people in this part of town had real jobs, and the jeans helped her to blend in. She'd needed to get away from the unreality of the beach and the villa, and she'd been drawn inland to the haciendas and working ranches that were part of a whole other Mexican tradition. An unseen world of cowboys and leather and horseflesh, where life was lived behind a pall of woodsmoke.

She stopped to lean on a metal rail and watch a man work a horse on a lunge-rein. The animal was calm and obliging, but she guessed it was still unbroken because it was bareback and wore only a halter instead of a bridle. Sure enough, the man brought the horse to a halt, walked over to it and spoke to it quietly before going to fetch a saddle from the corral's split-wood fence.

Across from Christine, some ranch-hands and kids were also watching the man. When he picked up the saddle, a thrill of anticipation ran through them. A kid who was sitting on the top rail climbed down to watch whatever was going to happen next from behind the fence, while two of the ranch-hands spit in their palms and shook hands. Christine didn't know the details of their wager, but there was clearly room for legitimate disagreement about how this was going to turn out.

The man carried the saddle to the horse, talked to it some more and then placed the saddle on its back. The horse tossed its head and snorted. Its front feet left the ground but only rose six inches into the air and then landed again. After a few uncertain steps, the horse stood still once more, but its rolling eyes betrayed an inner turmoil.

The man reached under the horse's belly and fastened the cinch strap. The horse stepped sideways, turned halfway round then settled. The worst was over.

The man paced out to the end of the lunge-rein and clicked the horse into motion. The horse bucked once, then trotted forward with the saddle on its back as though it had been saddle-broke forever.

On the other side of the corral, money changed hands.

"You like horses?"

She turned to see a man in a Stetson leaning on the section of fence next to hers. He was taller than her, and some years older. Wiry and attractive, without an ounce of excess fat anywhere on his body, he was wearing the sort of home-spun, sweat-stained jacket and pants that you'd usually only see on a respectable married rancher in a Western.

"How could anyone not love horses?"

"Beats me, but some folks don't."

He had an unusual accent that she couldn't place. She didn't think he was Mexican, but he was also unlike any American she'd ever met.

"The name's Valentine."

He was exactly like that cool drink of water that country singers warn people about in songs that Christine never listened to.

"Christine. Pleased to meet you."

She pretended to watch the horse that was now trotting neatly around the corral.

"You want to go for a ride, Christine?"

"Not on this one."

"How about them other horses yonder."

He indicated five or six ponies grazing in a nearby paddock.

"Those are yours?"

"Not yet."

"What does that mean?"

"It means I aim for them to be."

"You're going to steal them?!"

He stared at her for a moment.

"Pleasure to meet you, Miss Christine."

He tipped his hat and walked away. Christine was dumbfounded. And more than a little curious.

"What's wrong? Where are you going? Hey!"

She ran after him.

"Hey! It was you that started this, and now you're just going to walk away? What did I do?"

Valentine just kept on walking.

"I'm here to do an honest trade in horseflesh and I don't

take kindly to folks who peg me for a horse thief."

"You're kidding, right?"

"There's folks would still hang a man for stealing horses, and I might count myself among their number."

"Well I didn't mean anything by it. And the people I know, they'd never take offense at something like that."

"What people are those?"

"It's a long story, OK? Let's just say they can be pretty volatile."

"You've known some bad men?"

"I guess I have, yeah."

"It's good that you know it. It behooves you not to spend no more time in their company."

"I guess I was thinking pretty much the same thing."

Valentine finally stopped. He looked at her and weighed her sincerity.

"Then good luck to you, Miss Christine."

He tipped his hat again and made to leave. Christine grabbed his arm.

"Hey, come on. What about that ride you promised?"

"It was only an offer, it weren't no promise."

But he didn't walk away, and Christine knew she was going to get her ride.

As soon as they had ridden clear of the ranch, Valentine and Christine nudged their horses into a lope and set off toward the sage-colored hills in the distance.

She'd learned to ride before she reached her teens, and around the age of twelve, horseback riding had become something of an obsession. Being on a horse again now, for the first time in years, long-slumbering muscle groups stirred and remembered and awakened old feelings that were both familiar and pleasantly strange. She was a natural rider and completely at home in the saddle, which was just as well because Valentine would clearly have been impatient with anything less.

The man riding ahead of her lived by some code that she didn't understand. She didn't feel entirely safe with him, but that was part of his appeal.

She accepted – in fact she was pleased – that others thought her willful and irresponsible. But riding away with a man who had materialized at her side less than an hour ago took irresponsibility to a delicious new level. She told herself that if anything happened – she wasn't coy, but she didn't care to make the thought any more specific – it would absolutely not be her fault.

They rode to the edge of the flat country and slowed to a walk to follow a wide trail that led up into the hills. After twenty minutes of easy climbing, they reached a draw with cottonwood shade trees and a boggy, creek-fed watering hole which had lately been trampled by the hooves of countless heads of cattle.

They dismounted. Valentine took her reins and she watched him lead the horses to the clear water beyond the mud.

"You're not from around here are you?"

From the draw's elevation, Valentine gazed out over the coastal plain below like he was judging it.

"I only come down here when I have to."

"You don't like it? It's probably the best place I've ever lived. It sure beats the Northwest. That's where I'm from originally." He didn't even seem to be listening. Feeling like a fool, she tried again.

"So where do you live?"

"South. In the highlands. About a hundred miles beyond these hills."

"I didn't think there was anything down there. Is that still in Mexico?"

"I couldn't rightly say. It's not a question that's ever come up."

"Wait, you're saying you don't even know what country you live in?"

"I know we got all the water and timber we need, and the land is passable. Folks from the outside just leave us be."

"That's pretty hard to believe."

"I guess. It's not an easy place to live."

"You have family up there?"

"There's kin, but not close kin, not any more."

He seemed uncomfortable with the subject. Christine didn't push him.

Valentine removed his hat and shaded his eyes to read the bright but hazy sky. The sun was up there somewhere, but it was hard to say where.

"We got maybe two hours till sundown. No sense in lingering."

He held her horse while she mounted it. But then, instead of mounting his own horse, he stayed beside her stirrup, still hatless, and gazed up at her.

"Miss Christine, I don't want you thinking I don't know how these things are done, but I'll be headed home tomorrow, and I'll count myself a fool if I don't take this one chance right now to ask you."

You can't be serious, thought Christine. You can't possibly be serious...

"Ask me what?"

"If you'll come home with me."

She might have anticipated his mad proposal, but her jaw dropped just the same.

"As my wife, I mean. I don't mean no funny business."

For Christine, it was a strange journey home. On the ride back to the ranch, Valentine kept some way ahead, and left to her own thoughts, she began to wonder if the stress of the past few days and the nostalgic spell of horse riding might have caused her to hallucinate. It seemed incredible that the words she remembered hearing could possibly have been spoken.

But as he led her horse away and tipped his hat in fare-well, he'd added –

"I guess the churches in this town would all be Papist, so I hope a civil service is all right with you. I'd need your answer by morning."

Christine promised him she'd think about it.

The next day, Christine was woken by a pounding on her door. She noticed that her body ached in several places, but it was a good ache.

Emma stood slouching in her doorway with her arms folded.

"There's a man on a horse. He's asking for you."

Christine went to the window. Valentine was down there sitting on his horse. He was leading a string of three other horses, and there was a rifle in the scabbard that was slung across his saddle. The first horse in the string also carried a saddle.

"What the fuck have you been doing? Who is this guy?"

Christine pulled on some clothes and went outside.

Valentine tipped his hat when he saw her.

"Miss Christine."

"You shouldn't have come here."

"I'll leave if that's what you want. Is that what you want?"

Emma called down from an upstairs window:

"Hey, you. Crazy cowboy, yeah, we want you to leave. Like right now."

Valentine deferred to Christine.

"I need to hear it from you."

"Wait there."

Christine went back inside. She ran up to her room and hastily heaped together a pile of practical clothes. Emma watched her in amazement.

"Girl, you are not thinking this through. You don't walk out on Luiz. And especially not to run off with some crazy dude."

"I don't have a bag. You have one I can borrow?"

Emma fetched a bag. Christine stuffed the pile of clothes into it.

"That's Louis Vuitton, so you owe me big."

Christine lugged the bag to the door, where she stopped to give Emma a hug. Tears slid down Emma's cheek.

"Just how rich and badass did this guy tell you he was?"

"Goodbye Emma."

"Yeah yeah, that's what you're saying now. I just figure you got to be tripping balls. But what am I going to say to Luiz? If you're still gone when he shows up here again?"

"Tell him goodbye."

She gave Emma her cell phone and headed down the stairs.

"You want me to lie about where you've gone?"

"You'll only piss him off."

"What if he comes looking for you?"

"I'm walking off the edge of his world. He's not going to find me."

She went out to join Valentine.

They were married at noon. The ceremony was performed in a municipal building before the eyes of a non-denominational God, and it was quite moving in its way. The elderly female witness cried and the Judge was suitably impressed by the madness of the enterprise. Christine used her US passport, and Valentine had somehow made arrangements that prevented his lack of ID from being an issue. He'd also brought his rifle into the room and leaned it against the Judge's desk because, as he said, a rifle was not something that you'd want to leave outside and unattended.

As the couple said their vows, tourists snapped pictures of their horses, which Valentine had hitched to a metal barrier in the parking lot. The tourists loitered and speculated, and when at last the newlyweds emerged from the building arm in arm and mounted up and rode away, their progress was recorded in dozens of images taken by cheerful well-wishers whose names the happy couple never knew.

These faintly surreal experiences conspired to push Christine and Valentine closer together – and to exclude Christine further from what she had always thought of as the real world.

They rode at a walking pace all afternoon, and sundown found them deep in the same range of low hills where Valentine had proposed. They made camp near a small stream, but they lit no fire and pitched no tent and after a cold supper of beef jerky, it became clear that they were both going to sleep on the ground.

Valentine had a bedroll, but Christine only had the clothes she'd carried with her. The night was cold, and she slept fitfully, half expecting that Valentine would come to her as a husband to his wife. She was relieved – and slightly puzzled – when he did not.

The next day, she rose chilled and shivering in the pale light of dawn. Valentine was already folding up his bedroll. She wondered if he would have let her use it if she'd asked, and as she explored the fantasy of how that might have played out, she arrived at a sudden, sober understanding of her predicament: she had just gotten married to a man she was afraid of.

Valentine picked up his neatly folded things.

"We need to be moving."

"Some coffee would be nice."

"We ain't allowed no coffee."

"What, so you didn't bring any?"

"I didn't bring any because it ain't allowed."

"You've got to be shitting me."

"I'm telling you like it is."

"I guess I'd settle for a bloody Mary."

Valentine let that lie. He tied his bedroll to his saddle.

"Do you even know what that is?"

"I know close enough. We don't partake of alcohol nor smoke tobacco neither."

"So what, you're a Mormon?"

"I never heard that word. I can't say if that's what you'd call it."

"How many wives have you got?"

"What kind of a question is that?"

"I guess you're not a Mormon. Jesus, what the hell are you?"

He came over to her and grabbed her arm.

"I'm a God-fearing man who don't hold with that blasphemy you're speaking. You're my wife now. You'll want to mind me on that point."

He let go her arm and went back to his horse.

"We can eat later, after we've made some distance."

His words felt like an apology, and she was grateful for the concession.

As they rode out of camp, the sun broke clear of the high

ground to the East and chased away the shadows that pooled between the rolling hills.

For the first few miles, Christine was stiff and sore, but her muscles slowly eased with the steady sway of her horse, and her mood climbed with the sun. She was glad that the trail they followed was so easy because Valentine had impressed upon her that their itinerary was inflexible, and she didn't want to slow them down.

The day wore on, and they started to descend. The air was drier here, and the grass was thinner. Early in the afternoon, they came around the last hill and Christine gasped at the unexpected sight of a vast inland desert.

The sandy wilderness stretched out before them on a vast plateau and seemed to be devoid of life. Christine was overawed, and Valentine was pleased with her reaction. He betrayed a fatherly pride in the desert, as though he'd created it himself.

"It keeps the outside world outside."

"Is it completely barren?"

"It might as well be. There's things that live out there, but they won't let you see them."

"And we have to cross it?"

"You see those peaks?"

He pointed at a jagged bruise-colored smear that ran along the far horizon and which Christine had mistaken for a bank of clouds.

"How long till we get there?"

"All goes well, I figure on three days."

"What if things don't go well?"

"Then we won't get there at all."

Valentine hobbled the horses and built a small fire, which he started with a flint. He fetched a can of sardines in tomato sauce from his saddlebag, emptied the contents into a pan of water and set the pan on to simmer.

"That's got to be your own recipe."

"More or less."

Christine went to Valentine's horse and looked inside the saddlebag. She almost blasphemed, but managed to divert her exclamation into an obscenity that Valentine had indicated was acceptable.

"Holy fuck, that's all you brought!? We're going to be eating fish soup all the way across this desert?"

"Fish is hard to come by. I never even saw a fish till I was nineteen."

"Yeah. OK. You know it's kind of weird that you'd remember your first fish?"

"It was a salmon. It was chewed up some, but the man who brought it home said he'd seen it fresh caught and that he'd stole it from a family of bears."

"That's quite a story."

"We had no cause to doubt his word. And that salmon was good eating. I aim to eat them every chance I get."

"You know this isn't salmon, right?"

"The storekeeper said it's all they had."

"Are you bringing back a can for that guy? The one in the story?"

"Uncle Joachim ain't no longer with us. His arm was tore up pretty bad by the bears and he barely made it home. He died soon after."

He handed her a mug of soup and Christine ate it, or drank it, in silence. Apart from water, it was the first thing she'd consumed in thirty-six hours. It tasted pretty good.

After they'd eaten and scoured the pans with dirt, Valentine called for her to follow him. He led her to a rock at the edge of the desert, and showed her where a spring bubbled up and disappeared again into the sand.

He told her to fill her canteens because this was the only water he knew of until they reached the other side.

Christine told him she wasn't carrying any canteens.

This was a possibility that Valentine had failed to consider. He explained that although he could carry plenty of water for one person, he hadn't thought to bring any extra canteens now that there were two of them.

Christine was incredulous. And pissed.

"What, so you just forgot that we were going to be crossing a fucking desert?"

She didn't even want to think about the shitstorm they'd be walking into if they had to turn back now.

"The folks I know all carry their own water. It ain't something you have to tell them."

"Well maybe you should have told me because I didn't get the memo."

She stomped about in the sand and kicked at the pans that Valentine had brought to be rinsed. He watched her in amazement and thought of intervening, but he was afraid of making things worse.

Christine's rage eventually burned itself out. She still didn't see any good options, but they had to do something.

"If we go for it anyway, what are our chances?"

"We'd probably make it. As long as we're careful."

"Then fuck it, let's go."

The plan was to ride on for the few hours that remained until sundown and then make camp. Even by the light of a moon that was nearly full, it was risky to travel by night because the desert floor was treacherous and deceptively hard to see and the horses were likely to stumble. Besides, it wasn't crazy hot in the daytime, it was just that there wasn't any water.

But Christine had been running on fumes for too long. Now that she had eaten, the adrenaline that had kept her going finally switched off, and her body began to clamor for all the other stimulants it had been missing.

Dehydration was the least of her problems – she'd drunk as much water as she could from the spring at the edge of the desert – but it wasn't helping. She had a bad headache and worsening stomach cramps and she was jonesing like a mother-fucker for a hit of pretty much anything.

She felt like shit and she looked even worse.

"Hey, Valentine. Hey!"

She'd thought she was shouting, but even her horse had barely heard her.

She put her thumb and index finger in her mouth and blew a piercing whistle that got a reaction she didn't see be-cause she was busy falling off her horse.

When she recovered her senses a few moments later, she found she was somehow on her feet and clutching hold of her saddle. She was sweaty and shaking and feverish, and Valen-tine had his hand on her cold, clammy forehead. He offered her his canteen and she drank from it but she was drinking too much and drinking way too fast. Valentine tried to stop her but she pushed him away and chugged down another half liter before she threw it all up again. A wave of remorse and futility washed over her, and she held out the unstoppered canteen, intending to give it back, but instead she passed out and it fell from her grasp as she slid unconscious to the ground.

When she woke some hours later she was lying on her back on the cold ground, except that the ground wasn't cold, it was soft and warm, either because it was dry sand or because she was lying on Valentine's bedroll. She saw him sitting on the other side of a small flickering fire and tried to explain to him that he should go with her up to her room where they could do a couple more lines and have a good time and after that every-thing would be fine.

Then she remembered where she was and started muttering that –

"It was the fish. The damned fish. Must have had something in it that didn't agree with me..."

And then she briefly became alarmed at the implications of Valentine's failure to chastise her for her blasphemy, but she reasoned that he was sitting so far away that perhaps he hadn't heard or perhaps he had chastised her and she'd not been listening or perhaps she'd never even said the words out loud. She took this as evidence that her powers of reasoning had been restored and was so much comforted by this that she fell at last into a relatively peaceful sleep.

She awoke the next morning feeling very weak. She told Valentine she was well enough to travel, but although she drank a little water, she had no appetite for sardines in any form.

Valentine was anxious to push on, but he was also unconvinced by her protestations of recovery. He thought they should go back. On hearing this, Christine got up, walked to her horse and hauled herself into the saddle. The effort nearly killed her. She ached all over and it was a bad ache, an ache that comes from sickness, but she got her way. Valentine swiftly broke camp and they rode onward into the desert.

Christine had been counting on the sun to warm her bones and make her strong again, and it seemed to be working. Of necessity they moved slowly, but the miles slipped by one after the other, and Valentine judged that they were making fair progress. Around noon he proposed that they stopped to eat and to rest for a while, but Christine consented only to take a little water and insisted that they keep riding on. She was reluctant to dismount for fear that if she were once to lie upon the ground, she would not be able to get back up on her horse again.

So they continued on. They rode more or less abreast –

Christine always lagging slightly – and Valentine grew increasingly concerned for the corpse-like figure, pale beneath her sun-bronzed skin, who sat her horse beside him. But he had no better plan, and every step brought them closer to the relative safety of the massive Sierras that waited for them up ahead.

Christine for her part had no thoughts at all. She saw and heard nothing, and her entire existence was reduced to a single trance-inducing task: ensuring that the body she inhabited continued to respond to the motion of her horse.

As the light faded, that motion stopped and Christine once again became aware of her surroundings. She saw snow on the peaks of the Sierras, and heard the soft, soothing jangle of harness against the quiet of the desert.

Valentine made camp in silence. He'd picked the spot because there was a cactus growing there – the only one he'd ever seen in this forsaken place. He had no hope of finding water, but he cut pieces from the youngest cactus leaves and gave them to Christine. She gnawed upon them hungrily.

That night her sleep was troubled, but she slept through until morning.

The next day Valentine could see she was no better, but they'd come so far that now there was no longer any thought of turning back. This time he had to help her mount her horse. Christine did not know him or understand where she was, but her body complied with his instructions and he was relieved to see it still remembered how to sit a horse.

She'd eaten nothing since the cactus pulp, but he knew a man could go for many days without eating. The dehydration was much more serious, and she was still refusing to swallow more than a few mouthfuls of water.

And then beneath it all there was another, deeper sickness. Valentine had never seen a person in withdrawal, but even in his ignorance of chemical dependencies, he guessed the kind of shock that she was going through. Christine was young and strong, but he was afraid that the stress of all three conditions at once might prove too much.

It also seemed inevitable that sooner or later she would start to crave water, and his biggest fear was that he would not have enough. So when, incredibly, a thick fog closed in upon them halfway through the morning, Valentine came as near as he had ever come to a feeling of despair.

They had no compass, and it would have been madness to continue. Even after they had stopped, Valentine struggled against a queasy seasickness as the horses and Christine were swallowed up by the drifting fog, only to reappear again a few moments later in a slightly different location.

Everything was damp to the touch, but Valentine could find no effective way to extract more than a few drops of water from the vapors that swirled around them. From time to time, the fog thinned, and then he glimpsed bright sunlight overhead: fifty feet above them the air was still clear. He felt taunted, and half believed that God had sent this fog to punish them, although for what particular sin he had no notion.

They made no more progress that day. Valentine took it hardest of all. The patient horses merely waited, while Christine slipped into a merciful delirium in which she mostly seemed content.

The fog lifted in the night as though it had never been. In the hours before dawn, Valentine fashioned a litter from his bedroll, Christine's clothes and pieces of harness. At sunrise, he lashed two horses together side by side and secured the litter across their backs. He laid Christine on the litter with her head supported by the horses' hindquarters and her feet dangling between their necks. Valentine was uncertain if the litter would hold, so he went on foot before the two horses to lead them by hand, and they advanced even more slowly than before.

He figured that if they were going to make it at all, they'd have to complete the desert crossing within the next two days.

CHAPTER 4

It was a relief to reach the trees.

Darkness had overtaken them at the end of the second day before they'd reached the edge of the desert, but with only a few miles to go, Valentine had kept plodding on, and the rising moon found them moving up a gentle incline that was sufficiently fertile to support an occasional clump of grass.

Their water had gone, Valentine was exhausted and the horses even more so. But an hour later they made the tree line and half an hour after that, they picked up an animal trail that led them through the pine trees to a watering hole where there was also grass for the horses.

Christine was unconscious and cold to the touch, but still alive as far as Valentine could tell. He laid her on the springy ground and covered her, then fed and watered the horses. He drank his fill at last and tipped some water into Christine's mouth but it only dribbled out again. He made fish soup and ate it and then he lay down beside Christine and slept.

The next day Valentine awoke refreshed and the horses too were much recovered, but Christine's condition was unchanged. He cut boughs from the trees and built a rough shelter over the place where she lay – not so much to protect her

but to let her see, if she awoke, that she had not been abandoned. He had no more food, but he left her with a full canteen and tried not to think about bears and then he took all the
horses and rode out.

Christine lay there undisturbed for two more days. In the
evening of the second day, had she been awake, she would have
seen a small procession of torch lights coming down through
the trees toward her. She would have heard twigs cracking
under hooves and the squeak of metal springs and the steady
scrunch of two large wooden cartwheels upon the forest floor.

She would have seen Valentine and four menfolk from
his community and a careful nine-year-old boy called Mark,
who had begged to join their expedition and had promised only
to observe and not get in the way.

She would have felt Valentine – for he would not permit
the other men to touch her – lift her up and place her in a cart
that gently bumped along all through the rest of the night and
most of the following day until she would have sensed, perhaps, the sharp disapproving stare of a woman in late middle
age, before experiencing once more the sublime feeling of being raised into the air and placed this time between the coarsely
woven linen sheets of a large unmoving bed.

The bed where Christine lay was in one of the many
rooms inside Valentine's sprawling log-built house, and while
she lay there, the community – which consisted of about a hundred souls – absorbed the fact that Valentine had gotten married to an outsider.

The gossip was surprisingly subdued. Most people, men
and women alike, were naturally curious about the new bride,
but they could only shrug and wait to see how things turned

out. And if the disapproving woman denounced the marriage as an impetuous mistake, and proclaimed to all who'd listen that she called upon the Good Lord to summon betimes this importuning hussy to her final reward, still, the community as a whole was tolerant of Valentine's decision and the general opinion was that his choice of partner was "understandable".

This was the time of year when Valentine would usually have taken his two dogs and gone hunting, roaming on horseback across the wooded hills and valleys for days at a time, either with one or two other men or more likely on his own. But this year he strayed no further than the lower meadow, which he plowed and tilled in preparation for a winter sowing, and spent the rest of his time ensuring that the house and barn and other wooden outbuildings were ready for the coming winter.

At night he slept beside her and sometimes gazed upon her, but never touched her.

Several times, when Valentine was out working his land, he was alerted by the barking of his dogs. But he would hurry home only to find the boy, Mark, loitering in his vegetable garden or climbing in his fruit trees, and once he caught him peering through the windows of his house. He chased the boy away because he thought he ought to, but he also knew the boy was motherless and saw no harm or evil in his fascination with Christine.

The following day, after his morning school-lessons, the boy returned once more. He knew by now the location of the room where Christine lay, and how to spy on her without setting off the dogs.

Valentine was working in the barn when the boy came up behind him and tugged on his jacket.

"What is it, boy?"

"She's moving. The lady in your house is moving. Come and see."

Christine had awakened as easily as if she had merely been asleep. She sat up in the bed and at first she accepted her unfamiliar surroundings as a matter of course. But as she looked around the room she became increasingly aware that this was unlike any place that she had ever been. She felt that she had somehow been transported a hundred years into the past. When she tried to remember where she might be, she found her mind was waking up more slowly than her body, and the memories would not come. She also found it hard to account for the young boy who was watching her from outside the window with his face pressed up against the glass. But after a moment he ran away, and she thought no more about it.

She was hungry and thirsty and began to understand that she had slept for a long time – in fact for two weeks, as she was later told. She got out of bed and left the room in search of food and drink.

The bedroom was attached directly to a well-proportioned space that seemed to be the inside of a fairly large log cabin. There were rafters overhead, a fireplace with a stone chimney, and an area that seemed to serve as a kitchen.

She found nothing to eat in the kitchen except for bundles of herbs that had been hung up to dry. There was also no faucet, so she took a metal pail from among the pots and pans and carried it outside.

She'd expected to see a well or some kind of pump, but there was nothing. She stood in front of the cabin holding the empty pail and blinking in the sunshine.

Hurrying toward her was a man she thought she knew, and scuttling along in his wake was the boy from the window. For a mad instant, she wondered if this boy could be her own child – and then her mind came into focus and she remembered everything. She called out her husband's name:

"Valentine!"

She was wearing the sort of long, plain nightdress that a child's doll or modest fairytale princess might wear. But beneath the nightdress she was naked, and she could feel the heat of the sun on her body.

She thought that he was going to speak, but there was nothing to say. He swept her up and carried her back inside the cabin. It was the first time he had held her in his arms. She smelled his sweat mixed with the scent of freshly turned earth as he carried her across the threshold and on into the bedroom. He set her down on the bed. She stood up again and helped him out of his jacket as he pulled off his boots. He took off his shirt and she started to unfasten the buckle of his belt but he finished taking off his pants himself and then he laid her down on the bed and they made love.

The boy watched everything through the window, and he was still there when Christine woke up a short time later and remembered she was desperately hungry. She saw the boy and waved at him to go away but he would not.

She remembered this was her house now. One of her first domestic tasks would be to see about some curtains.

"Valentine, wake up."

She shook his shoulder. Valentine came awake, and when the boy saw him stirring, he ran off.

"I need to eat."

Valentine cooked stew while Christine drank water from the well (which turned out to be behind the building) and gnawed on jerky. After Christine had devoured the stew, she suggested going back to bed, but Valentine misunderstood her intentions and said that she had rested long enough. She saw that he was eager to show her around, and since she was curious to learn about her new home, she postponed sex and let him lead her around the property instead. They visited his orchard and he took her to the barn where the horses were stabled in the winter. He pointed out the smokehouse and the tool-shed and the trapdoor that led to the root cellar and showed her where the grain was stored.

She tried to take it all in. It was hard for her to see how she could ever be comfortable here, but she shrugged and figured it would work itself out.

There was only one immediate problem.

"What's with those dogs?"

"It's their job to bark at strangers."

"I'm not a stranger. I'm your wife."

It felt unreal to be saying it out loud. Back in Tulum, she'd taken Valentine as her "lawful wedded husband", but it was the Judge who'd bestowed upon her the title of wife. This was the first time she'd felt the weight behind the words.

"The dogs don't know that."

"Yeah, I know they don't. I was kind of joking. But they're smart, right? If they see me around here all the time, will they figure it out?"

"If"?"

"Or will you need to explain it to them?"

"You ain't just a stranger, you're an outsider."

"Really? That's what I am? You're not going to get all Dueling Banjos on me, are you?"

"I don't know what that means."

"It means your dogs don't know where I'm from."

She was surprised that Valentine thought for a moment before answering.

"I couldn't say. It seems to me they might."

The dogs stayed quiet enough when Christine was in the house, but later that afternoon, when she was in the kitchen trying her hand at doing the dishes in cold water and without any dish soap, the dogs started barking again in earnest.

Valentine came inside and told her there was a delegation of folks who'd come out from the community to pay a visit.

"A delegation? Shucks, for little old me?"

He was nonplussed by her reply and thought it best to explain.

"It ain't nothing formal, but you'd do well to dress up nice."

She was wearing jeans and sneakers and a torn, brightly colored sweatshirt. These were pretty much all the clothes she had left after Valentine had jury-rigged the horse-litter.

"I'm guessing this won't cut it, huh?"

She read the answer from Valentine's expression. He seemed genuinely distressed.

"I just had my butt dragged through the desert backwards. Won't they make allowances?"

"They surely would. But you're my wife now and they shouldn't have to."

With that he unlocked the door of one of the cabin's other rooms and went inside. He came out a few moments later, locked the door behind him and held out a purple dress with pleats and ruffles that might have been considered fancy back in Edwardian times.

"You want me to play dress-up? Seriously?"

"I'd be obliged if you'd put it on."

The dress was hopelessly dated, but it was well-cut too.

"Where did this come from?"

"Another lady. I reckon she'd have been about your size."

The delegation came to a halt outside the cabin, and the dogs' barking crescendoed. Christine slipped away into the bedroom.

Valentine opened the cabin door and greeted the man who stood in front of him.

"Good day to you, Nathaniel. It's good to see you."

"Good day to you. I've come here with these brethren," – he indicated the men and women standing behind him, who variously nodded, curtsied or tipped their hats – "to offer our congratulations and to welcome your new wife to our community."

"That's right neighborly of you. Won't you please come in?"

Pastor Nathaniel took off his hat and came inside. He was a young man, smooth skinned and dark haired, and he wore a black soutane. The others shuffled in behind him.

Nathaniel advanced to the middle of the room and cast his eye about expectantly.

"My wife will be right out."

Nathaniel nodded graciously as if to say there was no hurry, but even so, Valentine felt every second of delay, and when at last Christine condescended to flounce into the room, he was mortified to see that the bodice of her dress was still unfastened and she was clutching it to her bosom.

"Honey, would you do me up? I do declare this dress has more tiny buttons than you could shake a stick at."

The back of Christine's dress did indeed have many buttons. Valentine's fingers – usually so skillful – were unsuited to the task and it seemed to take forever.

"There! Thank you."

Christine curtsied to their guests. Although most of them naturally took her extravagant manner to be the custom in the outside world, they were uncertain how to respond. Valentine, however, was alarmed by the bizarre changes in his wife's behavior and speech. Since he had never seen a movie in his life, he failed to recognize her crude pastiche of an antebellum southern belle, and he feared she may have lost part of her mind in the desert after all.

Nathaniel on the other hand knew play-acting when he saw it, and was completely at ease.

"We heard that you were better, and I am very glad to see you well."

"I thank you, sir – thank all of you. You were informed correctly, for as you see, I am now very well indeed."

She went to Valentine and, standing dutifully beside him, she took her husband's arm and placed a wifely hand upon his shoulder. But the character she was playing inspired her to flirt with their guest, and she gazed shamelessly at the handsome young Pastor the whole time.

"Nathaniel here was of the party that bore you from the forest."

"Indeed?"

Nathaniel gave a slight, self-deprecating bow.

"Any man in the community would have done the same."

Christine nodded to the modest Pastor and acknowledged his contribution with a smile. She hoped her vague response was adequate. She also wondered what had happened to her in the forest and made a mental note to ask Valentine about it later.

Nathaniel became aware of Valentine's confusion, and to avoid embarrassing their host any further, he decided to keep their visit brief. He apologized for arriving uninvited and said they did not mean to impose.

The delegation took their leave, and once more Valentine and Christine found themselves alone.

They made love again that night after their visitors had gone. Valentine fell asleep afterward, but Christine stayed awake, staring up at the pinewood ceiling. There were shadows moving outside the window, and she wondered if one of them might have been the boy.

CHAPTER 5

Christine worked at settling into her new life. She had fled from her suburban home and moved to the city when she was seventeen, and she had not accepted Valentine's proposal because of any secret wish to go back to the land. On the contrary, the men and women of Nathaniel's delegation had served as cautionary examples of what she feared to become: a lumpen, dull-eyed, docile creature whose life became an endless series of joyless tasks all the way to the grave.

But despite her instinctive horror of all things rustic, she saw no option but to persevere. She found the days passed pleasantly enough. At first the very strangeness of Valentine's world kept her amused, and then, as novelty slid imperceptibly into habit, she experienced a certain satisfaction in exercising her new skills. She grew accustomed to the quiet rhythms of her life with Valentine, and her respect for his abilities grew.

He made love to her only on rare occasions. She would look at the makeshift curtain she'd strung across the window and think that it had hardly been worth the trouble, but she told herself she didn't mind. She wondered what would happen if she became pregnant.

She'd explained to Valentine her strange behavior on the night of Nathaniel's visit. Although he didn't understand it any better than he had at the time, he accepted her apologies and let it go. But when she asked him about the dress and the locked room, he grew evasive.

"I told you about the dress already."

"What else is in the room?"

"Things we have no need of."

"But the dress was useful, wasn't it?"

The dress had gone back into the room after she wore it, and although she had no interest in wearing it again, she had hardly any clothes. If there was a dress, there might also be something wearable.

Also of course, she was just plain curious.

Valentine hadn't answered her question. She pushed him further.

"If you say there's nothing useful in the room, then why would you keep it locked?"

"Because folks have no business going in there."

"Hello? I'm not folks, Valentine. I'm your wife."

"And I'm your husband, and I say we'll speak no more about it."

A few days earlier, she'd worked her way around the outside of the cabin – driving the dogs into their usual frenzy – and found a window that looked into the locked room. It was hard to see inside, but as Valentine had implied, it was mostly full of junk: old boxes, bits and pieces of broken furniture, something that looked like a birdcage... Still, she would have liked to open up the boxes and rifle through the musty drawers and cupboards.

There was no sign of the dress, but she remembered it had been in very good condition, which was in striking contrast to the other contents of the room.

With so little else to occupy her mind, she didn't think her curiosity was so unreasonable. She also hadn't expected Valentine to be so stubborn.

"Fine. I don't even know why you're making such a big deal about it."

The next day, she noticed that the room's window had been boarded up from the outside. She didn't bother asking Valentine about it because she figured that he wouldn't tell her and would only get annoyed. In any case, she knew that he'd been patching up parts of the house against the first storms of winter, so it was probably just a coincidence.

The snow came two weeks later. Overnight, the landscape disappeared, and far from transforming the world into a twinkly Christmas fairyland, everything beneath the lowering sky turned flat and gray and oppressive.

Christine had had her share of fevers, and she knew what "cabin" meant, but although she'd heard of cabin fever, she had no real idea of what it was. By halfway through the morning she was experiencing it, and it was already driving her crazy.

She'd been with Valentine for two months by then, and in all that time she'd never been more than a few hundred yards from the cabin. But now she was desperate to see the community.

"There's nothing there."

"There's nothing here either."

"The community ain't a thing. It's not something you can go and see."

"Fine. I don't care. Take me to wherever it is and let me not see it."

"There's a foot of snow outside and more still falling."

"That's why I need to go."

"You ain't making any sense that I can follow."

"Look, there's your people up here, right? Nathaniel and the others. That boy."

"You mean Mark? What's this have to do with him?"

"They all have to live somewhere."

"You want to go visiting? Look outside. This ain't no visiting weather."

"No, it's stay at home and go crazy weather. That's why I need to get out. I'm not talking about visiting. You've got kids, so you must have a school. And a Pastor, so there's a church."

"We don't have no church."

"Wow. Really? Like, not even a chapel or anything? Or maybe a mosque?"

"I don't know what that is."

"It was a joke is what that was. Shit, I was wondering why it was taking so long to get to Sunday."

"Sunday was a couple days ago."

"Yeah, I know it was, Valentine. No offense, but you really need to keep up."

"I figured you was joking again. I just didn't get it. I also don't get why you'd be so keen to go to school. You're a grown woman."

"OK, let's try it this way: is the school on a street or in the middle of nowhere?"

"It's next to the Pastor's house. He does most of the teaching too."

"And the kids? Some of them live nearby?"

"Some of them do."

"Great! Then let's go there."

"You want me to take you to go see a bunch of buildings where you don't have no business?"

"That's exactly right."

"And you couldn't have done this before it started snowing?"

"Shit, Valentine, that wouldn't have been half as much fun."

"You ever used snowshoes?"

"You have any skis?"

"Wait here a spell."

Valentine went outside. An overhang had kept the front of the cabin clear of snow, so the door opened easily.

Christine wiped the steam from a window and watched him disappear into the barn.

He came back inside a few minutes later carrying a set of snowshoes, an ancient coat made from the skins of several dead animals that looked like it would be extremely unpleasant even to touch, never mind wear, and an antique pair of snow boots.

"These were my grandpappy's. In his day I don't think they had no skiing."

The main drag of the community – as Christine thought of it – had for the most part been churned into a slurry of black mud and slush, and the flakes of soft wet snow, which settled and accumulated on every other surface, melted in a moment if they chanced to land among its icy puddles.

Although they saw no other people out of doors, Christine was impressed that the street had been so thoroughly trampled. Perhaps the community was not so slow and backward after all. Perhaps it was a hive of energy and industry. Those who had ridden or waded through this freezing mud must have had places to go, people to see.

"Where is everyone?"

In answer, Valentine pointed to the smoke that rose, barely visible against the lead-colored sky, from several nearby chimneys.

"They're with their kin, at home."

"So we missed rush-hour?"

"I'd say these folks had business they needed to attend to. You wait upon the snow, and you could be a long time waiting."

"Which one's the school?"

"That one."

Christine made a snowball and threw it at the school-house wall.

"You want to tell me why you did that?"

"Why don't you try it?"

"This is how you used to spend your time?"

"Come on. You know you want to."

"I surely don't."

"Do it anyway. Do it for me."

Valentine bent down and scooped up snow. He pressed it into a ball and threw at the school and watched it burst against the clapboard wall. It didn't leave a white mark as Christine's had done, and he felt unsatisfied. He stooped to gather up more snow —

A snowball hit him in the back of the head. It was so unexpected that for a moment he thought he might have been attacked by a bear. And when he turned and saw Christine in his grandpappy's animal-hide coat, he was not immediately reassured. It was only when the laughing bear-like creature threw another snowball and dodged away that he understood it was a game.

Even as a boy, Valentine had never spent much time in play, but a snowball fight is pretty hard to resist — especially when the only alternative is to become a target for someone else's snowballs.

Christine and Valentine ran and played like children, fall-ing and stumbling into drifts, dodging along the streets and lay-ing ambushes between the houses of those who lived at the very heart of the community.

Although their cries were dampened by the snow, they were still loud enough — and unusual enough — to bring several people to their windows.

Mark was lured from the overheated parlor of a ram-bling house that he shared with five elderly brethren, but after watching for barely a minute, he grew cold and went back to the parlor.

Miriam dismissed them even faster. The moment that she glimpsed Christine, she set her jaw and drew her shades and retreated to her hearth.

But from an unlit upstairs room in the school-house, Nathaniel had watched them since Christine's first snowball had thumped into the wall beside him and called his wandering thoughts back to earth.

He watched and longed to join them, for he understood the nature of their fight. He knew that they would soon be heading home together, flushed and bright-eyed, and he knew with jealous certainty – even if they as yet did not – that they would soon be making love more sweetly than they ever had before.

CHAPTER 6

The days grew colder and brighter. The air became breathtakingly clear and dry, and every night a hard freeze transformed the snow into countless tiny crystals of ice that sparkled in the morning sunlight.

Christine was contented. With the whole world slumbering peacefully under a white blanket, there was little for her to do, but her life in the cabin no longer felt oppressive. She filled her days wandering along the paths of packed snow that linked the cabin to the outbuildings. Sometimes she'd visit the horses in the barn, or even feed them if Valentine was away with his dogs on one of his all-day hunting trips.

By now she knew her way around the root cellar and the larder, and she experimented with the deer-meat stews that Valentine was fond of. If my home-ec teacher could see me now, she thought.

But her clothes were becoming a problem. She couldn't wear Valentine's second shirt forever, and apart from her jeans, which also wouldn't last much longer, that was pretty much all she had to wear.

At first they'd tried to solve the problem Valentine's way.

"Up here, when you want a thing, you either make it, catch it, or grow it, or else you do without."

He'd given her the skins of two small deer from his hunt-

ing expeditions, but for all his skill in the smokehouse, he'd
made a mess of curing the hides. They smelled bad – worse
even than his grandpappy's reeking coat – and there were places
where the skin had been shaved much too thin. Christine had
done what she could, but after several frustrating and abortive
attempts at cobbling together a sleeveless vest, she'd also decided that deer hide was a pain in the ass to work with.

Valentine didn't really see the problem.

"I don't see why you need no fancy clothes anyway."

"I'm not talking about fancy clothes. I'm just talking about
clothes. Don't you even have a thrift store or something?"

"We got no stores in the community."

"Well I don't see people up here going naked, so there
must be something."

Valentine went into the bedroom and came back with a
blanket from their bed.

"You could cut a hole in this."

"You're not serious?"

"Why wouldn't I be?"

"I'll rock the blanket if I have to, but you're not making
me wear a poncho."

"Ain't nothing wrong with a poncho."

"Then you go ahead and wear one if you want to."

"It ain't me that's clamoring for a new outfit."

"All you need to know is that I'm not going to stick my
head through a hole in a blanket. Not in this lifetime. Not
ever. Listen, if I die up here you can even bury me in that
fuckin' dress, just don't bury me in a poncho, OK?"

Valentine didn't reply immediately, and she was amazed
to see that he had suddenly become furious.

"What do you mean, if you die up here? Where the hell
else are you fixing to die?"

He stormed out of the cabin. It was the first time Christine had ever heard him blaspheme. She'd never seen him so
angry.

The next time Valentine went away on one of his hunting trips, Christine waited till around noon and then set out for the school house.

She'd timed her visit well. When she reached the main drag, classes were just letting out. A dozen or so well-behaved kids of various ages came down the school steps together and headed off toward their various homes. She spotted Mark among them, but he didn't seem to take any special notice of her.

There was no longer any mud. Everything was white and frozen now, and the dispersing children followed well-worn icy paths between the deep banks of untouched snow.

Nathaniel had already noticed her. He came out and stood at the top of the steps.

Christine raised her hand in greeting and made her way toward him.

"Those your kids?"

"Most of them. Jessica and Ruth were sick today."

"Are they always like that?

"Like what?

"So well-behaved. They kind of give me the creeps."

"You'd rather they behaved badly?"

"Depends what you mean by bad. I'd rather they just behaved like kids."

"Things are different here. Wouldn't you expect the children to be different too?"

"Maybe it's the way you're teaching them."

"Isn't that the whole point?"

"The point of what?"

"Of life. To raise our children to become the people we would want them to be."

"Yeah, I can see why they hired you. Are you going to

ask me in?"

Nathaniel stepped aside and, with a sweep of his hand, invited her to enter. He followed her inside and shut the door behind them against the cold.

There were desks and tables arranged in groups around the room, and a chalkboard that could be moved around on wheels.

"Wow."

"'Wow'?"

"I wasn't expecting a notebook on every desk, but this is pretty spartan."

"We don't have notebooks. If we didn't have chalk, I don't know what we'd do."

Christine wandered to the blackboard and picked up a whitish lump.

"Dude, this isn't chalk, this is a rock. You're writing with rocks."

"It was good enough for Abraham Lincoln."

"Lincoln? You know who he was?"

"More or less. It's just an expression. He was famous for being educated in a one-room school house."

"That's what I've heard. But how come you know so much about him?"

"It's thanks to President Lincoln that we exist at all."

"Good for you. It's good to know you're not all descended from Nazi war criminals."

"I don't know that word. But I sense that you don't believe me."

"Whoa, back up. You don't know 'Nazi'?! I mean, if you were Valentine then sure, but you're a teacher. You people must really not be big on history then, huh?"

Nathaniel smiled.

"The community has gone its own way for a hundred twenty years."

"Yeah, so you said. Since Lincoln."

"Will you let me show you something?"

He led up a flight of wooden stairs and into a room that reminded her of the locked junk room in the cabin. Sitting on a table there was an old, art deco radio that someone had connected to a generator powered by a treadle.

"You know what that is?"

"It looks like something my great grandparents listened to before they invented entertainment."

"You pumped that treadle with your foot and the glass things inside would light up, and after a while you could turn that dial and hear people speaking."

"You guys really don't get out much, do you?"

"It doesn't work any more. I found it when I was a kid and I snuck up here alone a few times until one day I was listening and there was a crack like a gunshot and a smell of burning and it never worked again. But I heard some incredible things. Music. Sounds I could never have imagined. And I had the impression that some men have left this planet and traveled into space."

"Are you really asking? Because I can tell you if you really want to know."

Nathaniel thought about it for a moment.

"You're right. You shouldn't tell me. It's just as well the radio is broken. I often think that maybe I should destroy it completely. There's nothing that we need from the outside world except to be left alone."

"As preachers go, you know you're kind of out there."

"I'm not a preacher, I'm a pastor, and I serve the community as best I can. And now that Valentine has brought you here, you're one of us. I meant it when I said that you are welcome, and I'll do what I can to help you, although I can't hardly imagine what it must be like for you, and I'm afraid it won't be easy for you to accept us as we are."

"This place is quite a trip, and it's a hell of a long way from what I'm used to, but you know what? Biggest surprise so far is I don't even miss my phone."

"That's a good sign?"

"It means I'm doing OK."

"I'm glad to hear it."

"Thanks. Now can I tell you why I came?"

Valentine was unhappy about Christine "sneaking off" to see Nathaniel, and even more annoyed when she told him that she'd asked the Pastor to help her find some clothes.

"It ain't no other man's business what clothes a man's wife wears."

"Oh please. Where I come from, it's called shopping."

"It's time you figured out you ain't no longer where you come from."

"That's pretty much what Nathaniel said. He also said he'd been looking for someone to help out teaching."

"I didn't have you pegged for no teacher."

"What did you have me pegged for?"

"You can teach all the teaching you want when we have kids of our own."

"I don't know why you're so pissed off. You'd rather I dragged my bare-assed butt around the community knocking on strangers' doors and asking if I could have their old clothes?"

"Your place is here and that's all I'm saying about it."

Christine wasn't crazy about the idea of spending her mornings with a bunch of kids, no matter how well behaved they were, and she hadn't planned to take Nathaniel up on his offer. But if Valentine was going to be such an asshole about it, she thought that after all maybe she just might.

On her first day as a teacher, Christine turned up at the school house just after first light. The school kept "monastery hours", by which Nathaniel meant that since the days were shorter in winter, so too should be the length of time the children spent in school. The entire community followed a similar schedule, and the workday varied according to the season. Regardless of the time of year, people only labored in the hours between sunup and sundown.

Besides, some of the older folks could remember years gone by when bear tracks had occasionally been seen even on the community's main drag. Waiting until sunrise so that you could walk to school in daylight was no more than a sensible precaution.

Christine was anxious. As a woman, she had sometimes felt vaguely guilty about her lack of interest in children, although mostly, if she thought about it at all, it made her feel privileged and liberated. She was more than happy to be living her life without hearing the insistent tick of any biological clock. But what if the children intuited all this and thought she was a fraud?

So she'd come to the school house early to ask for Nathaniel's advice. He thought about it as he erased the previous day's lessons from the blackboard, and then reassured her with a platitude: don't think of them as children, just treat them as people, and you'll do fine.

She was also unclear about her responsibilities.

"What do we teach them anyway?"

"Are you good with numbers?"

"What kind of numbers?"

"Fractions?"

"No. Why do they need to learn fractions?"

"Let's hope they don't. Although the book we have on elementary math seems to think they're important."

"What other books have you got?"

"An illustrated children's bible."

"And?"

"Some hymn books. But they have no stories, and without the music, the children find them dull. And so do I. We also have eighteen volumes of handwritten ledgers containing meticulous records of every meeting ever held in the first few years of the community."

"Have you read them?"

"Some of them. I don't inflict them on the children."

"You don't care about your history?"

"There was a town in Ohio that had two churches. One of the congregations felt that the other was running the town for its own benefit, so they sat down and wrote to President Lincoln. They claimed that they were being persecuted for their religious convictions and petitioned for relief. After the Mexican wars, they were granted a charter that gave them permission to settle in the newly annexed south-western states."

"Well, that explains why we're all living in Texas."

"They didn't seem to think too much of Texas, so they crossed the Rio Grande and just kept on riding. The idea of the promised land is a powerful one, and on the trek south from Ohio a lot of other folks had joined them. By the time they reached Guadalajara, they were more than fifteen hundred strong. They were well organized too. Once they'd made up their minds to go somewhere, they'd have been pretty hard to stop.

"What didn't they like about Guadalajara?"

"I think they liked it well enough."

"So why didn't they stay?"

"They did, but only for a few years. I get the impression that they weren't too popular with the locals, but their community was thriving, and no-one raised a finger against them. Not until Sancho Villa came along."

"Ouch. How did their petition-writing trick work out

with him?"

"Not so well. A big group of about five hundred people got away and fled into these mountains from the inland side. These must have been pretty hardy folk, but by the time they pitched up here, they were down to three hundred and twelve souls."

"Then what happened?"

"The survivors dug their heels in and kept their heads down, and they put up these buildings. After that I guess they ran out of ledgers. Or maybe they just lost their appetite for writing it all down."

A blast of cold air blew into the room as the children came in through the school door in a group. They hung back when they saw Christine. Nathaniel went to welcome them and drive them forward. He addressed them brightly.

"Come in, children, and meet your new instructor. This is Miss Christine."

He introduced each student by their name, which, except for Mark and the twins, Jessica and Ruth, Christine promptly forgot.

The children all looked very serious, and she felt them judging her. When she tried what she hoped was a friendly, encouraging smile, one the smaller children started to cry.

She drifted over to Nathaniel and spoke to him out of the side of her mouth.

"So...?"

"Sit over there with the little ones. They'll show you what to do. Just listen to them read. You'll soon get the hang of it."

As Christine had expected, when she got back home Valentine was pissed. He accused her of defying him.

"I didn't defy you. You just said you weren't going to talk about it."

"I said we weren't going to talk about it and that you weren't going to do it."

"That's not how I remember it."

Valentine seethed with frustration. He turned his hooded eyes away from her and said nothing more.

Christine guessed that he was jealous and knew that she was playing a dangerous game, but she experienced a certain satisfaction in making Valentine mad. She felt that he deserved to suffer because his suspicions were so completely unfounded. She was blameless. She was in the right and doing good. He was just being irrational.

The following day, after classes had let out, Christine left the school and set off for home.

A figure dressed in black come out of one of the buildings and stood in the road ahead of her. As Christine came closer, she saw it was a woman — a sour-faced woman in late middle age who stood in the middle of the path of trodden snow. It was clear that she had no intention of letting Christine pass.

"Did you want to speak to me?"

The woman raised a shaking finger and pointed it.

"You!"

"OK, look, what's this about? Is it the school? Is one of those kids yours?"

"You have no place here, and no right to teach our children."

"Yeah, I'm sorry you feel that way. I'm not even going to get mad because I appreciate you people have some weird ideas about how things work and maybe you don't even know how rude you're being, but you know what? It isn't up to you."

"Do not come to the school again."

"Come on, lady, if you really think that's going to work

for you, I'm done with this conversation. And I really hope you're not going to be pulling this shit every day."

The woman looked mean, but she also looked frail. With youth on her side, Christine figured she could get past her easily enough, but as she drew level, the woman screeched and grabbed her hair with a claw-like hand and tried to pull her down.

They staggered back and forth, both of them somehow staying upright as Christine struggled to pry herself free from the mad old woman's clutches.

"Stay away from the children."

"Get the fuck off of me, you crazy bitch."

The old woman clung on like death and the brawl might have gone on for hours, but Christine finally lost patience. She elbowed her opponent in the ribs and slapped her a couple of times and flung her into a bank of snow.

The madwoman looked up at Christine from where she lay, pale as a witch and spitting venom.

"You have no business living with that man. Get thee back to Babylon, you whore."

That afternoon, Nathaniel came out to the cabin. Christine let him in and he presented her with a bundle of clothes.

"What's this?"

"It's the best I could do. I hope there's something in there you can use."

"Thanks. But you didn't need to bring it all the way out here. I could have picked it up from school tomorrow."

"That's the other reason I'm here. I need to ask you not to come to the school again."

"Really? And why's that?"

"You know why."

"The madwoman? Or was it Valentine? And you're OK

with this?"

"It wasn't my decision."

"Oh well, so you're off the hook then."

"I did what I could. You're the first outsider here since – I don't know how long. Since before I was born. You make people very uncomfortable."

"That's good to know."

"Look, if you still want to teach, then maybe after a few years –"

"You really think I give a fuck about teaching? Or your fucking retarded kids? Just how stupid are you?"

"I should go."

"Let me ask you something, Pastor."

"What?"

"Would you call yourself an observant man?"

"Up to a point."

"Do you hear barking?"

"No."

"And did you hear any dogs when you came up to the cabin?"

"No, it was quiet."

"And why do you think that was?"

"Look, Christine –"

"Because the dogs aren't here, that's why. And why aren't they here? OK, I'll tell you: because Valentine took them out hunting. And here's the thing: why did Valentine go out hunting?"

"I don't know. He likes hunting. It's what he does."

"Yeah, we both know he likes hunting. But why did he go out hunting today?"

"What do you want me to say?"

"It was because yesterday we had this big fuckin' row. Well, it really wasn't such a big deal, but to Valentine I guess it was. And you know what made him so mad? He was jealous.

He was jealous of you."

Nathaniel stood frozen in the middle of the room. Christine walked right up to him. She spoke more quietly, in a different voice.

"He was jealous of you."

She reached out her hand and touched him.

A moment later, blind to everything else, they were in each others' arms, each devouring the other with kisses. A shared impulse swept over them, and almost without knowing how it happened, they found themselves in the bedroom.

As a lover, Nathaniel was not as accomplished as Luiz, nor as robust as Valentine, but – Christine paused to savor the old-fashioned word – he was certainly ardent.

Afterward, as they lay spent and satisfied, Nathaniel would have drifted into sleep, but Christine dared not let him. She shook him gently, kissed him.

"You must go."

Before getting up to straighten the bed, she watched him as he climbed back into his clothes. He looked surprised, like a man who had been woken from a furtive dream to find his secrets known to all the world.

When Christine walked into the school next morning, Nathaniel was already at the blackboard, and he continued the lesson in a painfully transparent attempt at nonchalance. The children were more forthright, turning in their seats and frankly staring. It was clear they knew that she was not supposed to be there. She hoped that that was all they knew.

She'd thought that Nathaniel might take her aside, or maybe even challenge her publicly, but the morning wore on and she resumed her teaching duties as a matter of course without a word being spoken. Even the children seemed content to play along, and the shock of her arrival slowly dissipated, until her presence once again felt normal and expected.

When school was over and the children had obediently filed out the door – albeit with more backward glances than usual – Christine and Nathaniel were left standing some feet apart in the empty school room. Without speaking, Nathaniel went to the door and barred it. He took her hand and would have led her up the stairs, perhaps to the room with the broken radio, but Christine stopped him.

"No. In here."

She made him fuck her up against a wall that was covered in the grubby hand-prints of generations of children, as battered desks and lumps of chalk and the melting icicles that hung from the eaves outside the high windows all bore silent witness.

She had grown reckless. She thrilled not only to the transgression but also to the idea of punishment.

"Will they make us pay?"

"They'll make both of us pay."

"What will they do?"

"I don't know."

But they made love every day that week, and the only change that Christine saw was in Valentine, who grew more taciturn than ever. She thought he might still be trying to think of a way to win their argument.

On Monday, after Christine and Nathaniel had been apart the whole weekend, they could barely wait for classes to be over. As the morning dragged toward its close, the air grew thick with lust, and even the youngest children noticed that their teachers both seemed more and more distracted. Christine began to wonder if they could not somehow arrange to make love before the class had ended. She longed to take Nathaniel to some shadowed corner of the room, where they'd tear each others" clothes off with the children still sitting at their desks, obedient and under firm instructions to keep facing the other way.

But then they became aware of a commotion outside. Someone had climbed up the steps in front of the school, and now they were beating on the door and grumbling indistinctly. Only when they started yelling did the words become clear.

"Begone from us, ye whore! Begone! Begone!"

Everybody, including Christine, gazed expectantly at Nathaniel. Outside, the shouting fell away – the old woman needed to catch her breath – but the banging continued, too loud to ignore. Nathaniel knew it was his place to act. He also knew Christine well enough to fear she might do something rash and irreversible. Seeing no alternative, he walked unwillingly toward the door.

He was halfway there when the door was pushed open and the old woman stepped inside. She scanned the room and spotted Christine, and then, instead of an accusing finger, she raised a shotgun.

"Miriam! No!"

Nathaniel rushed forward. The old woman was focused entirely on her intended victim, and she hardly saw him coming. He charged into her slightly from the side and knocked the barrel upward. Staggering from the impact and still clutching the weapon, she toppled backwards. But as she fell, the muzzle of the shotgun came back down again and the weapon fired with a roar so loud that for a moment everybody in the room was rendered deaf. But after the last echoes of the detonation had died away, there was still the sound of screaming from one of the children.

The screams were coming from Ruth. She seemed to have been hit in the chest, but there was a lot of blood and it was hard to see exactly where it was all coming from. Some of the children sitting near her had also been caught in the blast, although their injuries were relatively minor, and two of them found that they were not injured at all and had only been splattered by the blood of others. These two felt almost cheated, and in their confusion and relief, they were the only ones who cried.

Jessica stared at her twin sister in horror. Like everyone else, she had very little idea of what to do, and she was overwhelmed not only by tremendous sympathy for the pain that Ruth was feeling, but also by the terrifying conviction that an enormous distance had suddenly opened up between them.

Christine too felt overwhelmed. More than any of the other children, the twins reminded her of herself, and now she felt as if she'd simultaneously received a mortal injury and at the same time been left miraculously untouched.

Nathaniel was the first to do anything at all.

"Mark, fetch the doctor."

Mark obediently put on his coat and went out the door. The old woman was still crumpled on the floor, and as he walked around her – and around the shotgun that lay beside her – she reached out to grab him, but it seemed to be more in recognition or greeting than any attempt to prevent him from leaving.

They made Ruth as comfortable as they could. She was quiet now and seemed to be in shock. There was a large pool of blood around her, but at least it didn't seem to be growing, and when Mark returned with an elderly man who was – or once had been – the community's doctor, Christine took heart from the discovery that Ruth had been wearing not only her outdoor coat, but also several thick layers underneath.

Ruth's mother and father arrived. They waited stoically with grim expressions on their faces and watched the doctor staunch the flow of blood from their daughter's mangled flesh. When he was done, they asked him his opinion. The doctor refused to speculate on the girl's internal injuries or on the chances of infection, but he was confident that none of the pellets had penetrated all the way inside her. He helped them move their daughter onto the blanket which they had brought for that purpose, and assisted by Nathaniel and accompanied by Jessica and Mark, Ruth was carried home.

By this time, the other children had left, and the old woman had also disappeared, although strangely, she'd left the shotgun behind.

Not knowing what else to do, Christine went home.

She found that Valentine already knew about the shooting.

"I told you not to be no teacher."

"I'm fine, thanks for asking. Some little girl got halfway blown away, but otherwise there was no real harm done."

"It was you she came for."

Christine didn't feel even slightly guilty, but she had the feeling that perhaps she ought to, so she bit her tongue and let him have the final word. The whole thing had turned into a big mess anyway, and right now, silence seemed to be her safest option. She didn't want to accidentally let slip some detail she would rather have kept secret.

The next day she went back to the school. The affair with Nathaniel – and the charade of her teaching – all that was over, but she needed to speak to him. She tried to be as discreet as possible, arriving just before noon and intending to stay out of sight until she'd seen the children leave. But when midday came and went, and still no children appeared, she figured that school must have been canceled.

She climbed up the school steps and knocked on the door. She waited a long time, then knocked again. She looked around and saw no-one, but felt like all the world was watching.

She was about to knock again when she heard someone inside un-bar the door. The door swung open and Nathaniel stood before her. He looked haggard and morose. Christine was taken aback.

"Hi."

"Christine..."

She could see that he was carrying enough guilt for the both of them.

"Nathaniel, we don't need to have that conversation right now. That's not why I've come."

"Then why?"

"How is she?"

"She had a fever. The doctor says that's normal, but he doesn't say it's good."

"Will you take me to see her?"

"They're not going to want to see you."

"Maybe you're thinking of that crazy old lady. The one who shot their daughter. Maybe she's the one they're not going to want to see."

"Miriam is one of us."

"Miriam is a fucking psycho."

Nathaniel shook his head and managed to look even sadder than before. He started to close the door –

"Wait! OK, I know I shoot my mouth off but you've got to understand that it's a seriously weird setup you have here and it's just really hard for me to drink the Kool-Aid."

"If you want to be accepted, that's not the way to do it."

"Yeah, that's what I just said. Come on, Nathaniel. I'm not a bad person. I care about that kid and I want to see her. I had her name remembered and everything."

When Ruth's mother came to the door and found Nathaniel and Christine standing outside the family's large and well-kept home, her face grew dark with anger. She shared the general feeling in the community that even Nathaniel had been, somehow, partly to blame, and she had long ago conceived a frightened hostility toward Christine simply for being an outsider.

And now this interloper – who by her very existence had caused her daughter to be laying upstairs in the daytime in a darkened bedroom – had come here with her accomplice, the complicit Pastor, and was pleading for them both to be admitted.

Apart from Mark and the doctor, no-one else had thought to visit, not even the old woman, Miriam. But then why should they? Visits were of little use and there was no reason for Miriam to apologize. Ruth's horrifying accident was not her fault. The entire community wished for Christine to begone, and everybody understood that Miriam had good intentions. They regretted only that she had failed.

In a gesture of solidarity, Ruth's mother had even sent her husband to make sure that the old woman was given back the shotgun that she had left behind.

Meanwhile, the Pastor and the whore kept talking. Ruth's mother stood there blankly. She wasn't listening, but she felt badgered. They were taking turns to bludgeon her with words, and she thought that even if she closed the door, they would still be there when she opened it again, so eventually she stood aside and let them in.

They were shown up into the twins' bedroom, where Christine was surprised to find that Mark was sitting with the injured girl. He kept a solitary vigil – there was no sign of Jessica – and Ruth herself seemed to be asleep.

Mark was certainly a strange child. At school he'd behaved impeccably to the point of being bland, and Christine even wondered if he still remembered looking through her window. In any case, under the circumstances she was glad to let it slide. She nodded to the boy.

"How's she doing?"

"She's sleeping."

It was impossible to know if the agitated movements behind Ruth's closed eyelids were the result of dreams or distress, but her face was flushed and even without her injuries, the rough poultice that had been applied to her right arm and all the way down the side of her torso would have made it hard to lie down comfortably.

And a shotgun wound like that must hurt like hell. The very thought of all that pain made Christine wince. She wondered if the doctor had been able to give the girl anything like morphine — and before she could stop herself, thoughts of all the drugs she didn't have came flooding back. Her mind raced off on a sudden mad excursion: the doctor was old. He'd lived his whole life here, and must by now have picked up all there was to know about the natural pharmaceuticals that — Christine had no doubt — grew wild up in these mountains. Perhaps he could hook her up...

Christine forced herself back into the room.

"I hope she hasn't been in too much pain?"

The boy shrugged. He didn't seem to care if Ruth was hurting or not. Christine grew annoyed and tried to pin him down on why he was there.

"I didn't realize that you and Ruth were such close friends."

"We're not."

"Then why are you here?"

"Why are you here?"

Christine could have slapped the insolent little fucker. Her temper was already frayed after twenty straight minutes of the silent treatment from the girl's slack-jawed imbecile of a mother, and she really wasn't in the mood. She was just about to lay into him with a "what's your problem?" when Nathaniel intervened.

"Mark just likes to make himself useful, don't you, Mark?"

"Oh, I know that. I just wondered why he was here."

Nathaniel was shaken. He'd guessed that Christine had a vicious streak, but he was taken aback at the depth of her venom.

But the boy was unmoved. He looked at her coldly – which drove Christine to a fury.

"What would you like us to do, Mark? Should we leave you here alone with the naked unconscious girl? What do you say? Would you like it if we did that?"

She loomed over him. The boy didn't seem to care, but Nathaniel was afraid that she might strike him. He grabbed her arm and pulled her away and out of the room.

Christine was on a roll. She lashed out in all directions.

"The little fucker. You don't even know what he did. Or do you? Maybe you were the first person he told. You and your fucking delegation. You're all in this together, aren't you? You sick fucks."

Nathaniel set his jaw and dragged her out past Ruth's startled mother and down the stairs and on past Jessica – who now believed she'd seen two madwomen in as many days – and threw her out of the house.

Christine stopped raving, but now she looked almost feral. She glared defiance at Nathaniel, who stood blocking the doorway, and he was glad she wasn't armed. He wondered too if it might have been safer not to have let her go.

But Christine was done with Nathaniel and Mark and all of the rest of them. She went straight home and found Valentine.

"Take me hunting."

CHAPTER 7

"**B**ut you're a woman."

"Come on, Valentine, if you call yourself a hunter, that better not be your best shot."

"This ain't about how clever you can argue neither."

When Christine had come home and asked her husband to take her hunting, Valentine hadn't refused, he'd simply grunted in derision and ignored her. But now at supper — and it was a thin supper too, for Christine had decided that tonight she wasn't going to cook — she'd brought it up again. Truth be told, he had no real objection to the idea, but after Christine had ignored his express wishes about teaching and gone off to pursue her brief and humiliating career at the school, he wasn't going to let her off easy. He'd also come to think of her as frivolous.

"You ain't never shown no interest to go hunting before."

"Well I am now."

"You think you have the stomach for it? You couldn't hardly stand to share a room with them two hides I brought you."

"Valentine, they stunk. Stank. Whichever. They were carrion."

"Oh I know you're one to find excuses. I know that we'll be out there in the woods and that's when you'll remember all them excuses you brought along for why you need to go back home."

"I swear I won't."

"You will, and I'll tell you why. Because you're not a hunter, that's why. Heck, I don't even know why you're asking, because I know you don't really want to go."

"Look, you can go ahead and believe whatever you want. Just take me along."

Valentine sat for a moment, and Christine already knew she'd won. Sure enough, her husband got up and went out to the barn. She hoped that this time he'd come back with something better than his grandpappy's old coat.

He came back with a gun, which he laid on the table.

"Where've you been hiding this?"

"It's been in the barn."

"Was it your grandpappy's?"

"Reckon it's older than that. You know how to use one of these?"

"More or less. It's not one of those you have to load from the front, is it?"

He showed her the lever action, and how to load and fire it and make it safe.

"It's not as big as yours."

"This here's a varmint gun. It's enough to get you started."

"Will it stop a bear?"

"You shoot this at a bear, you better hope you miss, else you'll just make him mad."

"So, what? I'm shooting squirrels?"

"Squirrels and hare."

"I was joking! Really? You hunt squirrels?"

"I don't hunt squirrels, you do. I hit a squirrel with my Winchester, there won't be nothing left."

Valentine roused her just before dawn the next day.

"I seen to the horses. This here is your pack. Let's move out."

Christine rolled out of bed fully dressed and pulled on grandpappy's snow boots. She hoisted the pack and immediately decided that as soon as Valentine wasn't looking, she'd redistribute as much of it as possible to her saddle bags.

But when she went outside —

"Where are the horses?"

"I said I seen to them. I didn't say we was taking them."

"We're not riding?"

"Not this time."

He went into the dog-run around the side of the cabin and came back with his two hunting dogs on leashes. They were excited and barked even more madly than usual when they saw Christine. Valentine gave them a firm voice command and they immediately fell quiet.

"You want to show me how you do that with the dogs?"

"Wouldn't work for you. They're my dogs, not yours."

"You think you could teach them not to bark at me so much on this trip?"

"They're meant to bark at you. A dog gets confused if you try to make him follow more than one master."

"This is going to be fun, huh?"

They trekked through virgin snow for most of the morning. It wasn't exactly Christine's idea of easy going, but she didn't find it too hard either. She was getting used to the snow shoes too — which was just as well because there were no ready-made pathways of packed snow out here in the forests.

Under a flat white sky, they made their way beneath the pine trees and along the silent snow-covered valleys. The world out here was beautiful and still, and broken only by the sound of their breathing and the steady mesmerizing rhythm of their footsteps pushing one after the other across the frozen snow against the quiet jangle of the dogs' chains.

The woods were full of tracks, some crisp and freshly made and others old and blurred and fixed in ice like fossils. Many were made by the tiny feet of various small animals and birds, some were made by the easily recognized cloven hooves of deer, and one set of prints was the spoor of what Valentine identified as a species of big cat that was common years ago, although he said that no-one presently living in the community had ever seen such an animal.

Valentine spotted a squirrel. He stopped and hushed his dogs, then gestured for Christine to draw up level with him. The squirrel was up in the boughs of a dying pine tree just ahead. It was wary, but didn't seem particularly afraid of them. Christine raised her gun and fired – or thought she fired; the sound was so much quieter than she'd expected that she thought she may not have pulled the trigger after all – and the squirrel darted away.

There was no mechanism for adjusting the sights, so Valentine – who said that he had seen the bullet fly just below the squirrel's branch – told her next time to aim slightly higher.

A short time later thanks to his advice, she shot and killed a snow hare. He held back the dogs while she went to fetch it and she found that it was not quite dead. It was lying on its side and although she couldn't see where she had hit it, it was clearly dying and there were spots of scarlet blood nearby in the snow. She wasn't sure what to do. She thought that she should probably kill it, because while it showed few outward signs of fear or suffering, it would certainly be dead before very long, and a swift death at this point would have been a kindness. But she had never killed a rabbit with her hands, and in her innocence she was afraid of doing it wrong and making a horrible, painful, grotesque mess of the creature's last few moments on this earth.

So she picked the snow hare up and carried it back for Valentine to deal with, only to find that it had died in her arms. It seemed to have become smaller in death and its lifeless body struck her suddenly as infinitely pathetic.

"There's no need to carry it like that."

"Like what?"

"Like it was a baby."

He took it from her. He cut off its feet and head, and laid the body on its back in the snow to slit open the skin on its hind legs and belly so that he could tear its snow-white pelt clean off. He worked his knife into the stomach cavity and cut upward through the ribs to split open the chest, and then he reached inside and pulled out all the hare's internal organs until all that remained was something under a pound of bone and flesh such as you might see in a butcher's shop.

He threw the still-warm entrails to his dogs, and then he wiped his hands in the snow and held out the fur.

"Forty more of these, you'll have a coat."

He cleaned his knife and packed away the fur and the hare meat and they continued on.

Early in the afternoon, just after they'd rested for ten minutes to chew on jerky and swallow a few mouthfuls of water, they ran across fresh hoof prints and some deer droppings. Valentine picked up a dropping, smooshed it between his fingers and sniffed it. He told Christine that it was cold, but probably no more than two hours old and that the animal that produced it was a stag of maybe three or four winters. He also said that this was the animal they'd been loosely tracking, and that this was a good time to start following its actual trail.

Christine thought that he was full of shit telling her about the deer's sex and age from its droppings, and she immediately wanted to catch up to it to see if he was right. But Valentine said that deer spook easily and now that they were getting closer, they'd need to advance more cautiously. They started to thread their way through the woods more slowly than ever.

Christine grew impatient. She found their progress maddening, and with no deer in sight, she did not entirely believe that their frequent stops and pauses were really necessary. She became less and less interested in their quarry, and even started to suspect that Valentine had glimpsed the beast some time earlier and was just trying to impress her by pretending he could describe an animal just by smelling its poop.

My husband, the shit sniffer. Did that make his behavior endearing or just insane? Valentine had just raised his arm to signal another halt, and she stood stock still by reflex, as in a childhood game she used to play. She watched him listen. She'd noticed that you could tell he was listening even from behind. As usual, she heard nothing but silence. She waited for the game to start again, and tried to remember why she'd wanted to come.

When they came upon the stag – and it was a stag, with three-point antlers, as Valentine had predicted – it was as if it had materialized right there in front of them, much closer than she'd ever expected. She froze instinctively without being told to. The animal was nibbling its way across a patch of grass that lay hidden just beneath the surface of the snow. It seemed relaxed to the point of nonchalance, but they hardly dared draw breath as they waited for it to stroll forward so that the line of sight between them was finally broken.

The discipline of the dogs was amazing. Christine didn't know dogs, but these were tall and powerful and she guessed they must be some kind of hound mix. She saw now that this was what they lived for. They must have had the deer's scent in their noses for most of the afternoon, but far from any mad frenzy of barking, the second they saw the deer, they'd dropped to the ground immediately and even seemed to have muffled their breathing. Their eyes shone with intelligence and understanding.

And now Valentine sent them forward. In perfect silence, they slipped between the trees and vanished into the underbrush. Christine had no idea what would happen next, and Valentine, who crouched a little way ahead of her, was so intent upon the hunt that he seemed to have forgotten that she was even there. She pressed her back against a tree – and the physical sensation awoke an aching memory of being in the school room with Nathaniel just over a week ago when she was likewise pressed against a hard unyielding surface. In a panic, she banished the thought and out of respect for the stag, she forced herself to think about the mystery of death instead.

When she heard the dogs baying from somewhere beyond where they'd last seen the stag, she assumed that the quarry had somehow gotten past them and they were now running freely in some hopeless last-chance pursuit. But the baying was coming toward them, and in another moment she heard the approaching crashes of the deer. The dogs were driving the beast toward their master.

The blindly fleeing stag at last saw Valentine. It froze and stood at bay no more than twenty feet away, and Christine wondered why Valentine didn't shoot it. But then two hurtling shapes caught up and flung themselves upon the stag and brought it down, and both Christine and the stag now fully understood the nature of the trap in which the animal had been caught.

The dogs were tearing at the fallen stag's belly, and it would have been a long cruel death if Valentine had not stepped forward and plunged his knife into the dying animal's neck.

Christine had been anxiously watching the sun.

"Unless you know a shortcut, it'll be well past nightfall before we get back home again."

"We ain't going home. Not tonight."

"Valentine, it's the middle of winter. Can't we just put this up in a tree or something and come back for it tomorrow?"

Valentine had skinned the stag and rigged a frame to stretch the hide and had nearly finished field dressing the meat. The snow all around him was bloody and littered with un-wanted body parts, while his dogs sprawled incontinently with bloated stomachs and muzzles that were still covered in gore.

"You think I'm leaving this up in a tree just so's you can sleep in a proper bed?"

"But there's all this blood. Won't it attract bears?"

"It might."

"And anyway, won't we all just die of the cold?"

"The dogs won't. But we might."

He stood up with infuriating slowness and checked the sun and then took his time slinging the venison and Christine's hare up into a tree. Then he walked a little distance from the slaughterhouse and came to a halt on the lee side of an enor-mous pine.

"Bring me them packs."

Christine fetched the packs and Valentine dug out the snow from beneath the pine. He piled the excavated snow into a low wall as he went, and when he reached the pine nee-dles that covered the ground, he stopped digging and laid pine boughs over the hole as a makeshift roof.

Valentine had filled their packs with various animal skins, some of which had been loosely stitched together, and now he crawled into the trench-shaped hole and spread a large deerskin on the ground, fur-side up.

Christine crawled in after him. They lay down side by side and pulled the other skins on top of them and used the empty packs to block the entrance. They pressed against each other until each could feel the heat from the other's body.

Darkness fell, and the long cold night began. Christine felt like she was lying in a grave. She drifted in and out of sleep. From time to time they both awoke and thought about making love, but even Valentine was disinclined to do anything that might threaten the delicate cocoon of warmth where they lay huddled together so much more closely than they had ever lately done at home in bed.

When dawn broke, Christine was faintly amazed to find that she was still alive. She also felt extremely cold – far colder than she remembered being in the night. She panicked for a moment, afraid that she must have fallen sick, but then she realized that she was lying on her own: Valentine had already risen and taken his body heat with him.

She climbed out of the shelter and into a fresh new day that promised to be clear and bright with blue sky overhead. But there was also a thin, cold wind blowing in from the higher peaks to the West, and the forest was no longer still and silent like it had been the day before. She looked up and saw that the tops of the pines were swaying, and when the wind blew through the lower branches, it made them moan and sigh.

She found Valentine fitting both of the dogs with a travois so that they could each drag half of the deer behind them. He was anxious.

"There's weather coming in."

"How bad?"

"Bad enough so we don't want to get caught in it."

"Bad enough to miss breakfast?"

"I ain't playing around. Take some water now and dump the rest. Load up the packs and keep your jerky close to hand. Once we start we won't be stopping."

"Wait, dump the water?"

"You carry it if you want to, but if we die out here, it

won't be from thirst."

They hoisted the packs and set out a few minutes later. Valentine took the lead, with his two dogs and their loads of venison right behind him. Christine followed in their tracks.

"You're sure we're going the right way?"

She felt stupid as soon as she'd said it, and she was glad that Valentine didn't deign to answer. The wind that blew across their path was already getting stronger, and an ominous bank of gray vapor was tumbling over the peaks to the West and sliding down toward them like an avalanche. This was no time to be a wise-ass.

Christine had seen movies where a sandstorm blew in from the desert like an angry wall, and the blizzard struck in much the same way. It was like being attacked by a living creature: a howling gray tempest swept through the trees, bore down upon them and filled the world with stinging, white-flecked malevolence.

Visibility was reduced to almost nothing, but ahead of her, Valentine trudged doggedly on. Her smart-ass remark became a serious question now: how could he possibly know which way to go? What if he was leading them around in circles? Christine didn't even know if he had a compass – or how he would be able to read and follow it in these conditions.

The snow swirled around her ankles, and she strained to see the tracks that she was following. But she couldn't even see her feet, far less the ground she walked on, and every step became an act of faith. And then, when she looked ahead again, there was no-one there.

"Valentine!"

She screamed his name, but the wind snatched the word away from her. She wanted desperately to run after him, even in snowshoes, but in which direction? In such a constant horizontal blast of snow, she could hardly tell which way was up, and already she'd become unsure which way was forward.

Her body hungered for action, and yet she dared not move. The contradiction overwhelmed her mind and she stood frozen not from the cold or from despair, but from an almost mystical absence of all desire, even – or perhaps especially – the desire to live. Nothing seemed to matter. How absurd to struggle five yards further on when she might just as well die in the very place she stood! And in the spring they'd find her body – if they even came to look for it and if the bears had left it alone...

And then some part of her remembered the varmint gun. She unslung it from her shoulder, aimed it vaguely upward and squeezed the trigger. Did it fire? Had she remembered to re-load it? She touched the barrel with an ungloved hand but couldn't decide if it was hot or icy cold. She sniffed the breech and thought she smelled powder, but perhaps it was only the powder that had frightened a squirrel and brought death to a snow-white hare? And now death came for her, in the shape of two monstrous dogs, each one the size of a small horse, fol-lowed by the Grim Reaper himself, clothed all in black and looming out from among the trees. He called her by name:

"Christine!"

Death was harder than it looked. At the very least she'd thought she'd get to lie down, but here she was, plodding along through snow that still felt cold and wet and a wind that cut to the bone. She clutched hold of the leash that was in her hand and which was also tied around her body and kept following the two hell-beasts that she thought should rightfully be carry-ing her instead of the carcass of some dead animal.

She'd thought that it was already night, but then it grew darker and the blizzard still kept blowing and they walked on for what might have been three more hours and then they reached an open space and in front of her she saw what looked like a barn.

Valentine led her into their cabin and laid her in front of the hearth on animal skins that he took from their packs. He lit a fire and heated some water for her to drink. She said she was fine, really, she was fine. She'd been hoping to make it all the way home, but this place would do, and in fact it was just like the place she lived except it was different because dogs were never allowed inside their cabin and she would have noticed if they'd had two sides of venison hanging up right next to the chimney.

The next morning she really was fine. She felt a little disoriented – especially when she woke up and found herself on the floor – but that was all. It was like she'd been drinking, except that she didn't have a hangover and her head was clear. She was pleased to see that the dogs were gone and the venison was still there. Outside, the blizzard had finally blown itself out.

Valentine brought her a breakfast of fried deer meat, and after she'd eaten it she was overcome with tiredness. He helped her into bed, and as he left the room he said to her:

"We should do that again. You bring me good luck."

CHAPTER 8

Christine was very glad to learn that after several uncomfortable days, Ruth had pulled through and made a good recovery. She wanted to see the girl – to offer her congratulations, or her apologies, or really just to see her. She'd been sincere when she told Nathaniel that the twins were the two kids she liked best.

It seemed unlikely that Ruth's mother would want to let her in the house again, but Christine could also think of several reasons why a visit to the school wouldn't be a good idea either. And accosting Ruth in the street felt like it might lead to the kind of conversation – or confrontation – that neither of them would want.

So one afternoon, an hour or so after lunch, she went to the twins' house. When she got there she had second thoughts and wondered if it might be prudent to find out who was home and then wait, if necessary, for Ruth's mother to leave. But maybe she never left – unless of course there was some kind of emergency, such as her daughter getting shot...

Fuck it, thought Christine, and she marched up to the house and knocked.

She heard footsteps, and then the door opened a little way and Jessica's head appeared in the gap. She looked apprehensive.

Christine tried to keep it light.

"Hey Jessica, how you doing?"

"I'm well, thank you."

"Is your sister in?"

"What do you want with her?"

"I heard she was better and I wanted to see her. Listen, that thing that happened last time, with all the shouting? I'm sorry about that. It's just that I was really stressed out and I promise you it's not going to happen again."

Jessica considered for a moment, then she opened the door wide and invited Christine in.

"Which way?"

"She's in the work-room."

Jessica led the way to a room where Ruth sat at a mechanic's work-bench making adjustments to the insides of some kind of machine.

Christine had been expecting something more like a sewing room, and she was taken aback. There only seemed to be a limited number of tools – all of them dating from the nineteenth century – but the room was clean and well-organized, and she could see that the twins were both very much at home here.

"Ruth, I heard you were back on your feet again. I'm so glad. How are you feeling?"

"Much better, thank you."

There were still several ugly scabs and bruises on one side of her face. Christine figured they'd leave at least a few scars, but hoped they wouldn't be too bad. She didn't even want to think about what Ruth's body looked like.

"You know I'm so sorry about what happened. I just wish..."

"Yes, so do I."

"So, what are you making?"

"A clock."

"Another clock" said Jessica, and pointed to where there were already an assortment of working timepieces hanging on the wall.

"Wow! Really? You fixed all those?"

"Not all of them. Some of them we made from scratch."

The door opened and the twins' mother came into the room. She'd been about to ask her daughters, rather fatuously, if they had a visitor, but when she saw that it was Christine, she stopped dead and for a long moment she said nothing at all.

"It's fine, ma."

Ma was thankful that it would not after all be necessary for her to gather and express her complicated thoughts on the topic of Christine's presence. She could live with fine.

After she'd gone, Christine had an idea:

"Do you guys know what a radio is?"

Nathaniel had not looked pleased to see her. When he let her in, he looked like a man being forced to invite a viper into his school, and once the door was closed behind them, he was careful to keep a little further away from her than was strictly necessary.

Christine explained that she'd come for the radio.

"Did you even know the twins could do that stuff?"

"It's not that. You don't remember when I said that I was glad it was broken?"

"Well, now you can be glad it's getting fixed. Come on, Nathaniel. How is this not a good idea?"

"I'm sure they're very skilled, but something like this? It can't be possible."

"Not for you or me, but have you seen what they can do? They build their own clocks. It's like Switzerland in there."

They went upstairs to the junk room to take a look at the radio and the generator. In the cramped space, they stood quite close together, and they were both aware of it.

"It's too heavy to carry."

The radio alone was fairly massive, and the treadle for the heavy-looking generator was mounted in a cast-iron frame.

"We could drag it, but I know you've heard of wheels up here, and you must know someone with a cart."

"Do you really think they can get this working again?"

"If not, they can always use the parts to make a few more clocks."

The twins' father owned a horse-cart, and Nathaniel said that he would talk to him. Christine was afraid that he would freak out and shut the whole project down, but Nathaniel pointed out that her scheme was already presumptuous enough without also making it a surprise.

Nathaniel found that the father was glad to help. He was keen for his daughters to apply their talents, and felt bad that he had so far only managed to provide them with so few resources. By tacit agreement, the girls' mother was not consulted.

Nathaniel arranged for the father to bring his cart to the school the following day. When he arrived they discovered that the treadle had been bolted to the floor, which made it even harder to move than they'd anticipated. But eventually the two men got it up and maneuvered the whole apparatus down the stairs and out onto the waiting cart. The father clicked his horse into motion and drove away. Over the course of the winter, even on thoroughfares that were only rarely used, the snow had gradually become packed and even, and he met no difficulties on the short journey home.

There was no real need for Christine to go to meet the cart at the twins' house, but she went anyway. It almost felt like Christmas – and for all she knew, perhaps it actually was. She stood with Ruth and Jessica full of quiet excitement, and they were careful to keep out of the way as Nathaniel helped the father to unload the apparatus and carry it indoors. The twins' mother also came out to watch the introduction of this mysterious piece of machinery into the family home. It was hard to tell exactly what, if anything, she thought about the situation, and although Christine was grateful that she raised no objections, she judged it safer to let her be, rather than run any risk of provoking her with thanks.

After they had put the radio in the twins' work-room, the father had another surprise:

"Now, my girls, look what I found you up in the attic."

He showed them several hard-bound books and a few thinner volumes, all of them offering a variety of Illustrated Instructions and Explanations in the Art of Controlling and Manipulating the Electrical Flux et co. The girls fell upon these manuals with suitably Victorian expressions of delight. As they pored through the pages, Christine thought that some of the Illustrations looked suspiciously medieval, but she was confident that the girls were smart enough to figure it all out and find whatever it was they needed.

"I knew they were up there, but I saw no reason to fetch them down until now."

With the twins already happily absorbed in their new project, Christine and Nathaniel exchanged mutual thanks with the girls' father, and then took their leave. As far as Christine was concerned, the scheme was already a success. She also found she was content, perhaps for the first time in her life, simply to have done a good thing.

In the course of the following months, the girls' radio project made erratic progress. At first, Christine went to visit them every few days. She'd intended to give encouragement and to see how they were getting on, but they needed no encouragement and almost seemed to resent the fact that Christine thought they might. And on the technical front, once the radio had been removed from its mahogany art deco cabinet, she failed to perceive any further change from one visit to the next. The girls tried to explain what they were doing, and even asked her one or two technical questions, but it soon became clear that their understanding of the Electrical Flux was already far greater than their former teacher's had ever been.

And then one day Christine came into their work-room and found Mark sitting there. He didn't seem to be helping – in fact, he didn't seem to be doing much of anything, and Christine had no idea why he was there. It was unthinkable that he might have come out of simple friendship. She herself made an effort to be friendly, but as usual the little shit made no response. The girls didn't seem to mind him being there at all, but his mere presence was making Christine crazy. She found herself glowering at him – which of course he also ignored – and when the idea of physical violence started to become irresistibly attractive, she realized she had to leave.

After that, having no desire ever to see Mark again, Christine accepted the fact that this was the girls' project now, and she left them to it.

She surprised herself by going out on several other hunting trips with Valentine. He told her that a compass was useless if you didn't know where you were or where you were going, and she learned his trick of navigating through the forest by way-points and following contours. As he said:

"It ain't the shortest route, but the way these local valleys run, it's the surest."

And as she'd discovered, by moving steadily across a slope without going up or down, you could find your way safely back home even in a blizzard.

As they ranged further into the woods on their hunting trips, Christine started to wonder more and more about the desert that they'd crossed on their trek from Tulum. Since she'd been unconscious when she was brought into the colony, she had no memory of the last part of the journey and no sense at all of where the desert was. She only knew that it must lie somewhere below them, and her desire to see it became almost an obsession. Valentine said that in the winter, the desert was unreachable, but he promised her that when the snows had melted he'd take her up above the tree line and show it to her.

The days started to grow longer, but the world was still cold, and any water that the sun had melted froze again each night. And then one afternoon, just when it started to feel that winter might last forever, a storm rolled in that brought rain instead of snow. By the following morning, everything had turned from white to mud.

It was still raining hard, but for some reason that Christine didn't catch, it was important for Valentine to go outside and wade across his fields. She gazed out of the window and watched him get swallowed up by the downpour, and already she felt nostalgic for the crisp whiteness of winter.

She heard the dogs barking and wondered if they missed the winter too, and then she realized that someone was knocking on the cabin door. It was one of the twins.

"Jessica?"

"No, it's Ruth."

Christine had known it was Ruth from the small scars on her face, but she was suddenly struck by a generous impulse to pretend that they were invisible.

"What are you doing out in this weather? Do you want to come in?"

"No, I should get back to school. But the Pastor sent me

to tell you to come to see him after classes today."

"Why? What's going on?"

"He just said you should make sure you came."

Ruth was flushed – apparently from suppressed excitement, but it might also have been from the effort of tramping all the way out to the cabin through heavy mud in the spring rain.

"How's the radio?"

"You'll see."

And with that she was gone.

Shit, thought Christine. If Nathaniel wanted to talk to her – and about what? – why didn't he just come out to the cabin himself? And why couldn't he have asked her yesterday, before it started bloody raining.

She arrived at the school well after noon. Partly because she had been waiting in the hope that the rain might stop – which it didn't – but mostly because she just wanted to piss him off. But Nathaniel was waiting for her at the top of the school steps with a big smile on his face.

"Don't tell me you've been standing out here since school let out?"

"Come on."

He came down the steps to meet her and for a mad moment she thought he was going to take her hand, but he just swept past her and led the way down the street.

She splashed along after him.

"Where are we going? Can't we do it here?"

She followed him along the main drag to a large building not far from the school. As they drew closer, she heard music coming from inside. It sounded like some kind of traditional Mexican ballad, with guitars and brass underneath sentimental vocals sung by a light tenor voice.

"The radio!"

Nathaniel opened the door and stood to one side to allow her to enter ahead of him. It was a courtesy that seemed to spring naturally from the ambience created by the old-fashioned music, and as she moved on through the building toward the source of the sound, it was like dancing into the past.

The building itself contributed to the mood. It was dark and airless, and although it must have been built around the same time as the rest of the community, it seemed to have remained stuck in another century. It felt as though nothing new had happened there in the last hundred years. It even smelled old.

When Christine reached the large, faded parlor – complete with potted ferns and ornate plasterwork under its high ceiling – she understood why. This was the community's retirement home, where five of its oldest citizens lived in an unlikely menage with one of its youngest. And sure enough, there at the end of the room, next to the table that supported the radio – which now had a gramophone horn instead of its original internal loudspeaker – Mark was sitting next to the generator, pumping away on the treadle with both feet.

The parlor also boasted a wood-burning stove, and the home's five elderly residents were clustered around it with two or three other men and women who had come especially to hear the radio. An hour ago it had struck them with the force of a miracle – all of these people might otherwise have lived their entire lives without ever hearing any music at all – but it had quickly become an accepted part of their world. Already they were paying hardly any attention to the music at all, and the ballad's unintelligible Spanish washed over them half forgotten in the background. Even so, it brought new life and energy into the room, and inspired its occupants to dredge up joyful reminiscences from their younger days.

The miracle of the radio made quite an impact on Christine too. It was the first time she'd heard music since she left Tulum, and she found it impossible not to be moved by its rhythms and harmonies and by the sheer exuberance of the musicians – even in their rendering of this sentimental ballad. The sound quality was a long way from the high-end stereos that she was used to, but it had an identity all of its own, and it was real enough to reawaken a surge of powerful and sensual emotions that had lain inside her dormant and unsatisfied for too long.

"Do you see that horn?"

Nathaniel was at her shoulder. His face shone.

"It's new, right? I would have remembered something like that.

"It was taken from another musical machine."

"It's a good look. And a good sound too."

"When people heard what Ruth and Jessica were doing, they ransacked their barns and attics and brought them all manner of devices."

"And the twins put it all together. Good for them. Where are they anyway?"

"Ruth said that after they'd fixed the radio, they found they didn't care for the noise it made. But I think perhaps there was another reason that they didn't want to stay."

Nathaniel discreetly directed her attention to one of the visitors sitting near the stove.

"What? I don't recognize any of those people."

"Look again."

Christine looked more closely. Her jaw dropped. It was Miriam.

"You're kidding me. What the hell is she doing here? She shouldn't even be walking around."

"Christine, you need to understand. That may be how you do things in the outside world, but it's not our way here in the community."

"What, so there are no repercussions? Someone can go batshit crazy and shoot whoever they want and you'll forgive them?"

"Not exactly. And it isn't always easy. We just try to do what's best for everyone."

Miriam had been aware of Christine's arrival the instant that she'd come into the room, and now she was equally aware that the younger woman was staring at her. She twisted around in her seat and stared back. Christine was aghast, but Nathaniel merely nodded to the mad old woman, and after a moment she turned back to her neighbor and continued gossiping.

"Well, it's the first time she hasn't attacked me, so I guess it's working gangbusters."

The music on the radio came to an end and the pause ran longer than usual. Conversation died away. An expectant hush fell. The only sound was the squeak of the treadle as Mark kept grinding on with the steady patience of a donkey turning a millstone. Then a bossa nova started up and a thrill of excitement ran through the room. There was also a sense of relief. Conversations picked up where they'd left off, and with even more enthusiasm than before.

It was still raining hard when Christine returned home vicariously delighted by the twins' success, and enormously satisfied that her scheme with the radio had turned out so well. For the first time, and only provisionally – she couldn't even decide if this was cause for celebration or alarm – she also felt that some day she might after all become an accepted member of this half-assed, godforsaken community. For all her vocal skepticism on the topic, even the problem of Miriam no longer seemed completely intractable.

As she came around the corner of the cabin, she was looking forward to seeing Valentine and telling him her news.

She was puzzled to see a strangely shaped mound on what she thought of as the cabin's front yard, and even more puzzled when it lumbered toward her through the mud and rain. It took several seconds for her brain to process the visual information and tell her that she was being attacked by a large brown bear.

She couldn't remember if she was supposed to run or play dead, but even without the bear, she'd be putting herself in real danger of drowning if she threw herself down in the rivers of mud, so running was the only option that could be seriously considered. She would have loved to run inside the cabin and bar the door behind her – and maybe come out a few moments later to heroically drive the beast away with a flaming torch snatched from the fire – but even the most optimistic assessment would put the bear between her and the door five paces before she could reach it.

Simply running away, or even running away in the hope of finding Valentine, looked like it would be a good way to help the bear work up an appetite before it caught up to her and tore her to pieces, but as a course of action, it otherwise seemed to have little to recommend it.

The only thing she could think of was to seek safety from the dogs – the same dogs that still regarded her as an intruder – but why were they so quiet? Had the bear already killed them? And then she realized that they were in fact barking fit to raise the dead, but she'd grown so used to hearing them that she hadn't even noticed.

The bear was no more than ten yards away when Christine turned and ran. She unlatched the gate to the dogs' run, and would have closed it behind her, but the mechanism of the latch was complicated and the bolt was slippery from all the rain and she was distracted by the large bear that was bearing down on her and emitting a bellowing whine that was so unearthly she wondered if the beast might be rabid. She almost laughed to think that she was about to be killed by a hydrophobic bear who was only acting so mean because he was pissed off about all the rain. But she choked down the hysteria before it took hold and eased backwards away from the bear and into the zone that was controlled by the chained-up dogs.

The dogs were magnificent and terrifying and as game as any animal Christine had ever seen. There was never any question that they would rather die than yield an inch to the bear, which was nearly twice their size and swiped at them with paws as big as their heads. But every time she thought the bear was leaving, it only changed its mind and lumbered back again. And it would only take one lucky swipe and then there would be just one dog – and after that there would only be Christine.

The boom of Valentine's gun was almost as unexpected and hard to interpret as Christine's initial sighting of the bear. But although she was briefly puzzled by the sound, the dogs knew it instantly, and the bear felt an explosion of pain that made it turn and charge in fury at its new tormentor.

Through the sheets of rain and from where Christine cowered behind the dogs, it was hard to see what was happening between Valentine and the bear, but she knew that he needed to reload his rifle before he could fire again – and it was taking far too long. He should have chambered another round by now, and she should have heard that second shot...

When it came, it was followed by another pause, and then:

"Christine?"

She staggered out of the dog run and ran to him. She was shaking all over and grabbed hold of him to stop herself from falling.

"Did the dogs take any hurt?"

She could hardly think straight.

"No. No, I don't think so..."

He left her for a moment and went into the run to calm

his dogs and satisfy himself that they were uninjured. One of them had two long raking scratches on its shoulder, but the wound looked clean and didn't seem to have done much damage apart from tearing open the skin.

Valentine came back to Christine and took hold of her more roughly than she would have liked and led her into the cabin. They had to pass the bear, and she shrank back as they skirted around it, half afraid that it might somehow still be alive, but then she saw that Valentine's second shot had blown away almost half of the beast's head, and she was chilled and overawed and relieved all at the same time.

As soon as they were safely inside, Valentine took off his soaking hat and coat and dropped them on the floor. He did the same with the animal-skin coat that Christine was wearing and then pulled off his boots.

"What about the bear?"

She had no fear or interest in the bear now that it was dead, and she didn't even know why she asked.

"The bear ain't going nowhere."

He took her into the bedroom, and Christine began to feel a rising panic. She was still willing enough to make love to him again – she even wanted to – but not now, not like this.

"Valentine, no. Please don't."

The almost uncontrollable lust that she'd succumbed to in the early days of their marriage had long since withered away. In its place, celibacy had grown into a comfortable habit. By now they'd had no sex for several months, not since the shooting at the school.

He threw her onto the bed and climbed on top of her.

"Please, no. Can't you just hold me? I just want you to hold me, and then maybe in a while..."

She said the words out loud, but not to him. She had no hope that he would stop or that she could make him listen. She made the words and spoke them only to distract herself from what was happening.

She was trembling and crying, but he didn't seem to mind or notice. Maybe he even liked it. When he was done, he rolled off of her and fell asleep.

He lay there in a heap with his back to her, and she thought about what he'd look like with half his face missing.

CHAPTER 9

If the winter had been unusually long, so the spring, now that it had finally come, was correspondingly short. As the weather grew warmer and drier and more settled, Christine returned to her old childhood passion of horseback riding. She would wait until Valentine was already safely engrossed in his labors out in the fields, and then around mid-morning, she'd head out to the barn, saddle up one of the horses and ride out into the woods.

She didn't go very far, and she didn't feel the need to. There were days when she wondered what would happen if she just kept riding. Would Valentine regard her as a horse thief and come thundering after her, fully supported by all the apparatus of the law, as he conceived it? Or would she just be elevated to the mysterious and privileged rank of madwoman and thus be left to wander as she pleased?

But these considerations formed no part of any secret plan, nor did they arise from any conscious desire to escape. Mostly she just wanted to be alone – or to be more precise, she just wanted not to be in the community, even if it was only for a few hours. So she was content to turn around and ride slowly back home again in the middle of the afternoon in plenty of time to prepare Valentine's dinner. After all, she knew that she could always come back out again the following day.

The inevitable changes in her domestic arrangements with Valentine had been subtle. When he rose at first light, as he did each morning, she would now pretend to be asleep, and she'd stay beneath the covers until she'd heard him leave the cabin. Through the day, it was easy enough to avoid him, and then at night, when he was already exhausted from his labors in the fields, she'd make sure he ate a full dinner and say nothing when he rose from the table and disappeared into their bedroom. And even then she'd still stay awake for hours because she needed to be certain that he was sound asleep before she'd dare to slip into bed beside him.

Although he'd said nothing, she figured he must know that she was taking out the horses, but she didn't know if he'd noticed how little time they now spent together: they sat at the same table to eat their dinner – sometimes, if he remembered, Valentine might say grace, but these would be the only words spoken – and they lay each night unconscious for several hours in the same bed, facing away from each other and away from the unbridgeable gulf of maybe twelve inches that lay between them.

From her daily rides, Christine grew increasingly familiar with the local forests and valleys, and although she was discovering how each piece of woodland had its own unique character – boasting perhaps the towering skeleton of an ancient pine, or a grove of birch trees where the light was a softer, paler green – she also saw that every corner of the vast forest was essentially the same. Hungry for a new experience, she thought of Valentine's unfulfilled promise to take her above the tree line, so one day she set out earlier than usual with the intention of climbing as high as she could and at last seeing the desert for herself.

She started out along a deer-track that led into the next

valley and which she'd followed many times before. From there she turned her horse into the pathless woods and rode it up to the crest of the ridge. The climb was easy enough but the horse already sensed that this was not going to be one of their customary rides, and it grew restive. Christine soothed the animal. It trusted her and soon settled, and for the rest of the morning they rode steadily uphill along the top of the ridge.

She'd chosen this particular ridge because it was one of the longest and she guessed it would have an easier grade, and also because it projected furthest from the flanks of the range. She reasoned that this should give her the best chance of seeing the desert no matter how far around to the north or south it lay. But as they rose higher and the trees began to thin out enough for her to see beyond them, she was dismayed to see how the forest below extended out to the horizon in all directions. It was clear by now that the ridge they followed was indeed the highest for miles around, and since Valentine was not a man who'd say that you could see the desert from above the treeline if in fact you could not, she began to think that the vantage point he spoke of must after all be more than one day's ride away.

But she needed to see for herself. She was not going to turn around now, not after coming all this way.

When they left behind the last thin stand of scrubby trees, her horse became uneasy once again. She remembered how Valentine had persuaded their reluctant horses to leave the rolling grassy hills behind and step into the desert, and she followed his example: instead of trying to soothe the animal, this time she showed it her determination, and gave it no choice but to carry her further up the flank of the mountain.

The grade along the crest of the ridge was still easy enough, but without any vegetation, the landscape had become harsh and unforgiving, and instead of pine needles or even packed dust, the ground they walked on now was rock-hard and flinty. It was too much to ask of any horse, but there was no place to leave it, so Christine dismounted and slipped the reins over its neck and led the animal by hand. They continued to ascend higher and higher, and as they climbed, the ridge widened out, so that after another two or three miles, they were walking up a rocky slope.

The slope led up to the very foot of the mountain, where it ended in a jumbled wall of fallen rocks. The air up here still smelled of winter, and Christine realized that they were nearly at the snowline. Looming above them, she saw the same snow capped peaks that she had seen from the floor of the desert. She turned to look back the way they'd come, and far away to the north it seemed that just beyond the trees, she could almost see a strip of – something.

She needed to go higher.

Not very much higher. Maybe even fifty feet would be enough. The rocks were clearly impossible for the horse, but for a human they were only dangerous and difficult.

She found a place where she could wedge the horse's reins between two rocks and hitched it there as best she could. The animal seemed more settled now – perhaps it understood that this was as far as it would be asked to go – but Christine still stayed with it for another moment. She reassured it and only half in jest she told it it was free to work itself loose and return home by itself if she wasn't back within an hour, and then she began to scramble up the giant fall of rocks.

The most difficult thing about climbing up the rocks was knowing that she'd have to climb back down again. On the way up she could see which way to go – where to put her feet and where to reach when she needed a handhold – but when she looked back down again, the place where she had just been standing was not always visible, and she'd have to lean out further than she wanted to just to see the rock she'd come from. Searching for a foothold when she knew the rock was there was bad enough, but doing it blindly as she tried to pick her way back down – when the rock she needed to see wouldn't always be there – felt like a recipe for panic.

And as she clambered higher, she also discovered that simply looking down at all was an increasingly uncomfortable experience. She was only halfway to the ledge she'd picked out as her destination, and already it was a terrifying drop down to her tiny horse far below. She solved the problem by forcing herself to only look upwards, and hoped that the memory of each individual rock that she scrambled over would somehow come back to her in reverse order when she made her way back down again.

At last she crawled up over the final rock and hauled herself onto the ledge. She rested for a moment on her hands and knees, and when she'd caught her breath, she stood up before turning around – she figured the extra few feet of elevation couldn't hurt.

And there below her, far away, a few points to the east of due north, vanishingly small and yet unmistakable, she saw the desert.

It was flat and featureless and seemed to have no color, although beyond it she could see the mildest tint of greenish blue, which she thought must be the strip of grassy hill country that separated the desert from the coastal plains, and which had taken them two days to cross.

There was no horizon in that direction, only a dazzling blur of sunlit white from the pall of dust and pollution that hung above the lowlands. But the whiteness was also partly due to sea-haze, and she realized with a thrill that the air that she was gazing at must have drifted in all the way from the Caribbean.

In every other direction, except for one or two lost clouds

wandering over the forests far below her to the south, the air was crystal clear. She could see the curve of the earth. Before her, to the east, there was only forest, while everything behind her and above her was rock and snow.

And then, in the skies to the west, she saw an airplane. It disappeared and reappeared again behind the unpassable peaks. It left no vapor trail, and soon it was gone, but Christine suddenly understood why she'd taken so much trouble to come all this way. It had never really been about the desert at all. She'd needed to see – to see for herself and be certain – that she was still living on a world that was full of people.

She didn't want to rejoin them, she just needed to know that they were there.

Climbing back down was difficult. For one thing, she seemed to have somehow gotten onto a different route right from the moment she'd lowered herself over the edge of the ledge. She thought she recognized all kinds of distinctive markings and patterns in the rocks, but their relative arrangements were different, and none of them were in the places that she thought they ought to be.

It was also a little unsettling not to be able to see her horse. But it hadn't been visible from the ledge either, and she was confident that she'd see it again as soon as she'd climbed far enough down.

Meanwhile the immediate business of surviving the descent was more than sufficient to keep her occupied. Most of the time her blindly groping feet would find a foothold, but there were times when she lowered herself further and further until it was impossible to pull herself back up again, and still her flailing feet touched nothing but air – a deeply unpleasant sensation that dragged her back to the night of the blizzard, where the white-out meant stepping forward onto ground she couldn't see. But this was worse because, unlike the forest floor, here there could be no guarantee — or even expectation — that there would in fact be another rock to land on when she let go of the rock that she was clinging to and committed to the fall.

One time, tired of staring at gray rock three inches from her face, she thought she'd turn around and slide over a relatively easy-looking boulder on her butt, but it was an experiment that she only tried once.

By the time she reached the bottom, she'd badly jarred both ankles and strained one of them. She'd also wrenched her arm, torn all of her fingernails and somehow scraped the side of her face, which stung like crazy. But she was down.

The thing was, she'd come down in a different place to where she'd gone up, which wasn't the best news, because it meant that before she could get the fuck out of there, she still needed to find her horse. But it was a horse after all, a full-grown paint, so how hard could it be? And if she found it quickly, then maybe they could still make it all the way back to the tree line before nightfall.

She walked, or limped, along the foot of the rock fall in both directions. Everywhere looked the same and it took her half an hour to find the place where she'd wedged the reins — or at least to find a place that looked just like it — but there was definitely no horse. With the flint-hard ground, there wasn't even any sign that a horse had ever been there.

"I was kidding, you bastard!"

She yelled the words and although they didn't seem to carry, she hoped the damned horse would hear them and come crawling back full of apologies and with its tail between its legs. She wasn't too worried about the animal — she figured it had gotten loose and was halfway back to the cabin by now — but she was seriously pissed at herself. She'd screwed up badly, and surviving a night in the forest at this time of year without dying from exposure wasn't going to be easy. Then she realized with a sinking feeling that the horse had even taken her coat, which she'd left tied across the saddle.

Half an hour ago, even with all her injuries, this had still been a jaunt. And even when she'd first seen that the horse was missing, her immediate thought had been that hiking all the way home on a bad ankle was going to hurt like hell. But now she realized that was the least of her problems.

She set out down the slope, a speck of life painfully retreating from a towering mineral world of gray, limping toward a vast green forest without so much as a stick that she could use to help her walk. But at least the grade was constant, and after a while she came to an arrangement with the throbbing pain from her ankle: the deal was that the ankle would continue to hurt like a motherfucker with every step, while she pretended it was happening to someone else.

She reached the ridge, and that was easier. Or not exactly easier, but staying on top of the ridge required more focus, and she welcomed anything that could distract her from her present pain – not to mention from her imminent rendezvous with death in the forest.

And then, ahead, the first stand of trees. And amid the trees, there stood a horse. A paint, saddled and bridled, with a coat that was very much like hers tied across the saddle.

The horse had been hitched to a tree, and when she saw this, she became almost uncontrollably angry.

She took several minutes to calm herself down before she trusted herself enough to approach the horse without spooking it. Then she mounted up – which she had to do from the off-side because of her bad ankle, and which unsettled the horse all over again – and although she felt a furious urge to gallop, she rode the horse at a walking pace through the gathering dusk and into the forest and kept it moving forward at a careful walk all the way home.

Four hours later, Christine limped into the cabin leaning on a pitchfork that she'd found in the barn. Valentine took note of the pitchfork and he took a moment to gauge Christine's mood, but he didn't seem too concerned by either one.

"It's late. I stayed up special. There's supper."

"You bastard. I thought I was going to die."

"You could have."

"So you followed me up there and saw the horse got free – or did you lead it down there yourself? – and then you just turned around and left?"

"If you wanted me there, you could of said. Looked to me like you chose to go by yourself."

"Just because I don't want you for a fucking tour guide doesn't mean you can leave me up there to die. What if I'd never made it to the horse?"

"Then I figured to go back up tomorrow and fetch it home myself."

"Holy crap, Valentine, don't you understand? I was nearly dead before I even saw the fucking horse. Keep your supper. I'm going to bed."

"You're my wife, Christine."

"Not tonight I'm not. You stay on your own side of the bed."

"That's not what I meant. I meant that's my horse and I'm glad to let you use it. But you need to remember that I found you and I saved you from that bear and I carried you out of that desert. You belong up here now, and you belong to me. That's the way it is and you need to be clear on that."

CHAPTER 10

The next morning Christine woke late. Valentine had apparently already gotten up and gone out to his fields, although she wasn't even sure that he'd come to bed at all because the covers on his side had been neatly straightened up as usual. The sun was shining and for a moment all she knew was that she was glad to be alive and in bed and alone, and all she thought about was breakfast. But when she tried to climb out of bed, the knowledge of all the other details of her life returned with the throb of her ankle. It was still hurting badly, and it had swollen even more during the night.

She wondered how hard it would be to find the doctor who'd treated Ruth – the one with all the arcane knowledge of the region's psychotropic plants – but then she hobbled out into the main room and saw the pitchfork propped up by the door, and she realized that even the best doctor in the world would only tell her to do what she was aiming to do anyway: keep her weight off the foot.

She also thought how typical it was of Valentine to have picked up the pitchfork from where she'd dropped it – and how unlike him to then forget to take it back out to the barn. Or was he making a point? Or perhaps he'd even left it there for her convenience? Yeah, right. She grunted scornfully. Valentine occasionally made mistakes, but when he wanted to make a point, he wasn't the kind of guy who'd leave it open to interpretation.

She leaned on the pitchfork and made her way out to the barn, where she rummaged around among the tools. She found a rake that was about the right length, so she wrapped straw around its teeth and then used strips of rag to bind another clump of straw to the head and when she was done she had a serviceable crutch that would hold her up and also be good for scaring crows.

Mostly, while her ankle was healing, she just tried to walk around as little as possible. But a bad ankle didn't stop her from riding, even though it meant she freaked out the horses every time she mounted from the wrong side.

She had no intention of riding any great distance, and when she realized that even after all this time, she'd still only seen very little of the community and very few of its people, she decided not exactly to go visiting, but at least to go sightseeing. So she'd turn her horse away from the woods and ride back to the main drag and from there she'd follow any likely looking track and see where it led.

She'd take her makeshift crutch with her on these expeditions, just in case – she didn't plan on dismounting again until she was safely back in the barn, but you never knew what might happen. And as she rode around the wider neighborhood of the community with the straw-wrapped rake sticking out of her rifle scabbard, and with her newly finished coat – stitched together from the winter fur of sixty-odd small animals – tied across her saddle, the thought crossed her mind that perhaps she might be going native. But what if she was? Wasn't that what she was supposed to do?

She'd never paid too much attention to rural life before – or to any life except her own – but as she rode around, she watched whole families out working on their parcels of land, and she imagined them behind the walls of their log cabins and wooden houses, and she wondered how they lived.

And then one afternoon, when her unofficial survey of the community was nearly complete, she saw that she too was being watched. She took it to be innocent enough at first – some curious, bashful child perhaps, spying on her from the underbrush near the family home – and even when the watcher fled guiltily away, she only rode after him to reassure and to allay any fears he might have of getting into trouble. But the boy did not want to be caught, and she realized with some confusion that instead of fleeing to some nearby cabin, he was running hard and trying to make it all the way back to the main drag. And then, although she'd still not clearly seen his face, she knew that it was Mark.

She noted with some surprise that she wasn't even angry, but seriously, what was it with that kid? And was someone so sneaky really going to be so obvious as to run home to the place she knew he lived?

Apparently he was. She pushed her horse into a trot and judged she had a fair chance of getting there ahead of him to cut him off, but he must have known some shortcut because as she came in sight of the building, he was already running up the steps.

She hitched her horse to the rail outside and took her crutch, and made her way into the gloomy lobby. There was no sign of life, and no answer when she called out, so she limped on through to the parlor in back. The radio was still there at one end of the room, but there was no-one working the treadle, so it just sat patiently in silence – as it had done for so many years – waiting to be brought back to life again.

The rest of the room was so dark and quiet and still that she thought it was empty, but then she saw that there were three elderly residents dozing around the unlit stove like left-over witches around an empty cauldron.

"I'm looking for the boy. Mark. He lives here, right?"

The witches came awake. Two of them anyway. Just as it had been for her, it was something of a struggle for them to register that there was someone else in the room.

"Mark?"

"Yeah, hi, I'm Christine. I was here before for the thing with the radio. I need to talk to Mark."

The sleeping witch spoke:

"Upstairs. Second on the left."

"Thanks."

"He might not let you in. He don't let us in."

Second on the left turned out to be some kind of closet, but behind the third door on the left she sensed movement. Or a lack of movement. But there was definitely breathing – she could hear the breathing of someone who'd recently been running.

She would have tried to walk in, but she knew the door would be locked and she didn't want to give him the satisfaction of seeing her fail, so she just knocked.

"Who is it?"

"Mark, you know who it is. I'm not mad, just let me in."

The key turned in the lock and he opened the door a fraction.

"What do you want?"

"What do you think I want? I want to know why you're spying on me – again."

"I'm not spying on you."

He tried to close the door, but Christine was ready for him.

"Oh for fuck's sake."

She pushed in past him – which wasn't easy because even

though he was only a kid he was doing a good job of blocking the door with his foot; it was like he'd been practicing – and came into the room.

"Look, I get it. You're nine or ten or whatever and we all do weird things when we're that age. Well, not as weird as the creepy shit you do, but I've got to tell you, you need to stop foll- Holy fuck! What the fuck is all this?!"

It was a large room and her focus at first had been on Mark, so she hadn't noticed that behind the door, there were hundreds of dead cats piled up carelessly in a heap so enormous that it formed drifts where it ran up against the walls. Some of the cats had been attached to pieces of wood or nailed to branches in grotesque parodies of lifelike poses, and a few of them still seemed to possess some kind of internal skeletal structure, but most of them had just been skinned and indifferently stuffed and then just tossed – there was no evidence of any kind of display or intentional arrangement – onto the heap with the others.

"It was a pastime."

He fetched a book and presented it to her as mitigating evidence: A Practical Guide to Taxidermy. It was from the same century as the twins' Electrical Flux manuals.

"Listen to me, this may be what people did for fun a hundred years ago, but even up here – and I'm not even going to ask you how those cats died – this is not what you should be doing."

"I don't do it any more."

"Well, that's good, because it's sick. Do you understand what I'm telling you? And what about those old folks downstairs? Do they know about all these dead animals you've got up here? – Hey, Mark, are you even listening? What the hell are you doing?! Get away from me!"

The boy hadn't exactly gone into a trance, but he had moved uncomfortably close to her and he was clearly no longer paying any attention to what she was saying.

"There's a life inside you."

Christine wasn't sure if she'd struck him or not, but even if she couldn't remember how she'd gotten out of the room, here she was hobbling further away down the street with every step and that was the main thing.

She pitched up outside the school house, and for some reason instead of simply knocking on the door, she felt the need to call the Pastor out.

"Nathaniel! Hey, Pastor Nathaniel! I need to talk to someone, and you're it."

The Pastor came out from the school and gazed down at her with an expression of concern and bewilderment.

"Christine, how are you? What happened to your foot?"

"Yeah, right. As if you don't already know."

She hobbled up her third flight of steps that afternoon, pushed past Nathaniel and went inside.

He followed her and closed the door behind them and waited for her to compose herself.

"OK, Pastor, I have some questions."

"What about?"

"About one of the kids who comes here every day. The creepy one."

"Mark?"

"Yes, Mark. Pretty easy guess, huh? I was just in his room."

"Did he hurt you?"

"Why? Did you think he might?"

"Did he?"

"He seriously freaked me out is what he did."

"How?"

"It's quite a list."

"All right."

"For starters, he lives on his own with a bunch of old people."

"You knew that already."

"You don't think that's weird?"

"Yes, of course. His living arrangements are unusual."

"Do you know how he's been spending his time? Have you seen his room?"

"No."

"It's full of cats."

"Ah. That doesn't surprise me."

"It surprised the fuck out of me."

"For a time, Mark was very interested in taxidermy."

"No, see, that's not an interest, and it's not a pastime. It's something closer to genocide."

"I don't know that word."

"Come to think of it, I don't think I've seen a single cat since I got here. Dogs, sure, but where are all the cats?"

"Do I really need to explain?"

"Explain what?"

"That he's capable of being very single-minded when he applies himself. With the cats, he was very thorough."

"You're telling me an eight-year-old killed every last cat? Exterminated every last one in the whole community? And no-one even tried to stop him?"

"He has a relationship with death."

"Wow, OK. Now he has a 'relationship with death' – whatever that means – and you're OK with that?"

"What do you want me to do?"

"I don't know. But something. You're supposed to be a man of God."

"God also has a relationship with death."

"So you really are some kind of smart-ass Pastor after all. But that wasn't the answer I was hoping for."

"Christine, did you know that since Mark started living there, none of the residents have died?"

"You sure about that? I was just up there, and with two or three of them it was pretty hard to tell."

"That's the point. They're old, they're worn out. When people move into that house, they have nothing to live for and they're just waiting to die. It's the only thing that anyone expects of them, and it's all that they expect themselves. How do people like that keep on living for year after year after year?"

"I don't know, Nathaniel. Sometimes people just do. Sometimes people get to live a long time anyway, and no-one needs to sacrifice a fuckton of cats to buy them a few more days above ground on this shit-hole planet."

"Look, you're right. I think it's true that death fascinates him, even attracts him, but he also has a gift, Christine."

"He doesn't have a gift and he's not Jesus. He's a kid with a sick mind living in a fucked-up community that indulges him. And you know what? That's not healthy. The little shit shows way too much interest in my private life too."

"What do you mean?"

"You really don't know?"

"Why would I?"

"He looks through windows, OK? And he follows me."

"Well, in a way at least that's understandable."

"I don't want to understand him, I just want the creepy cat-killing pervert to leave me the fuck alone and stop spying on me."

"Christine, you're his mother."

"OK Pastor, you're really starting to piss me off now. Because — let me think — no, I'm pretty sure I'm not his mother. I'd definitely remember something like that."

"Not his real mother. His step-mother. The boy is Valentine's son."

Christine rode home in something of a daze.

Nathaniel told her that Valentine had been married before – it would have been even more of a surprise if he'd had the child out of wedlock – but that his first wife had died. The general feeling had been that the marriage was a mistake. The late Mrs Woods had been – and here the Pastor had looked away and chosen the word carefully – willful, and as an orphan with no other living family, she'd let the farm that she inherited fall into disrepair.

Christine became curious to see the place where her predecessor had lived as a girl and then grown up alone after her parents, her uncle and a younger brother had all died. Nathaniel told her how to find it, and on the way home she added a couple of extra miles to her normal route so that she could ride past it.

It was a parcel of land that Christine had ridden past several times before without paying it much attention, but now she saw that the tangled thicket of briars and vines that stood on a bare, stony patch of ground had grown up around the collapsed remains of a fair-sized log cabin. With the whole forest to choose from, it seemed willfully perverse that anyone would have chosen such a barren piece of earth upon which to carve out their home, and the entire plot was now so forlorn and derelict that it was hard to imagine that a family had ever lived there.

Christine already knew that Valentine was a solitary man who went his own way. Now she saw that his marriage to the owner of this property could not have brought him any material advantage. She also figured that he must have a thing for outsiders.

And what of his relationship to the boy? His own son! It was impossible for him not to know the boy existed, but in all this time he'd said and done nothing. What was keeping them apart? Was Valentine ashamed and trying to forget, or was there some secret he was trying to conceal? Christine wondered how a father and son could become estranged in the first place, and how long ago the break had occurred. Would Valentine still recognize his son? Did he even know his name?

It all seemed so unnatural. And yet it wasn't as if she felt any burning desire to drag Mark from the retirement home and force him to live with them in the cabin. She already had enough problems without that. And after all, if the community could respond by just shrugging its shoulders and accepting the situation, then maybe she ought to do the same.

But that night in bed she lay awake and stared at the man lying unconscious three feet away from her, and she wondered how many other secrets he might be hiding. She wondered once again about the purple dress and the dead woman who had worn it, and she wondered about the locked room with the boarded up window.

And she also wondered if that little shit could possibly have been right about the baby.

CHAPTER 11

"**Y**ou need to explain this."

It took a few moments for Christine to come awake and understand what was happening. Valentine stood in the bedroom doorway with some kind of bundle in his arms. It was easy to see that he was pissed, but she had no idea why.

"What is that? Is that a bunch of clothes?"

"I found them concealed in the window seat."

"Then they must be the clothes the Pastor gave me. And I didn't conceal them anywhere, that's just where I put them."

"You took clothes from the Pastor? After I expressly forbid you?"

"Well maybe I got them before you expressly forbid me anything. I don't remember. Come on Valentine, what's the big deal? I forgot I even had them. And anyway, I didn't take them, the Pastor brought them out here himself, so what was I supposed to do?"

"He come out here and met with you alone?"

"Well, yeah, I guess he must have."

Valentine left and closed the door after him. Christine lay back down with an extravagant sigh, still not understanding what had made him so mad. She'd almost fallen back to sleep again when she heard the sound of hammering outside the bedroom door.

"Valentine, what the fuck are you doing?"

"That man ain't welcome in my house."

"OK, great. I'll turn him away next time. But you know you let him in yourself."

"That was official business. It don't mean he gets to come out here and see you on his own."

"He's a fucking Pastor."

"He's a man in a hat. It don't make him no Pastor."

"Do you have any idea how much of an asshole you sound right now?"

Christine got up out of bed and went to open the door so she could argue with him face to face. But the door wouldn't open.

"Are you for real? You've actually nailed me in? Because you know what, Valentine? You haven't thought this through. Like for instance, where are you going to be sleeping tonight? On the couch? I mean, that would be great except, oh yeah, we don't have a couch."

"When I tell you do a thing, you mind you do it. I told you that before. I let you go free "til now and never asked no more from you than what a man is owed by his wife, but you had your own ideas about that. Well, now I'm telling you to stay put, and I mean to make sure you do."

"God almighty, Valentine, what the hell are you talking about?!"

"I told you not to speak that way. I know what I know is all I'm saying."

She heard him walk away after that, and when his footsteps had faded, she tried the door again. But it was so securely fastened that she soon gave up any hope of forcing it. She went and sat on the bed feeling helpless and frustrated, and tried to find reassuring ways to reinterpret his threats and insinuations. But the situation was so preposterous that even now she still felt very little real anger or even fear. She just figured she was in for a long, boring day, and promptly drifted into an idle fantasy about the things she'd do and say to him when he let her out to make his supper.

But when a sudden half-darkness fell over the room and she realized he was nailing a board over the window, she became seriously alarmed. She'd toyed with the idea of somehow climbing out that way, and although it wouldn't have been easy – the panes were fixed and it would have involved breaking the glass – it was comforting to think that she could always escape at any time if she really needed to.

And now that emergency exit was being closed. When Valentine nailed up the second board, the room became almost completely dark and she was truly frightened. Instead of plotting minor revenges and smart-ass remarks over supper, her fantasies also instantly grew darker: what if he were to leave her walled in here forever? What if he burned the place down? She wondered how much hard evidence or knowledge he actually had of her affair with Nathaniel. Was it possible that the Pastor had even been talking to him? Or had he spoken to the boy?

She passed a miserable day. She felt too vulnerable on the bed, so she dragged off some of the covers and wrapped them around her and squatted down on the floor with her back wedged into a corner of the room.

Then she remembered that she needed to pee, and when her eyes had adjusted to the dark, she groped around under the bed and pulled out the pot that was always kept there. She knew Valentine had used it sometimes in the winter, but until now she'd never used it herself because she'd always thought it was disgusting.

When she was done with the pot, she didn't know what to do with it. It didn't feel right just to push it back under the bed – she was also afraid that if it was hidden away again, she'd forget to empty it – but she also didn't want to leave it out on the floor where she might easily stumble into it. The problem was trivial but also insoluble, and even after she'd tucked it into another corner, she found herself haunted by the smell – or was it only the imagined smell? – of her own piss, and it nagged at her all day.

She also had no food or water, but she was too scared to be hungry and only felt thirsty when she thought about it.

Meanwhile on several occasions throughout the morning, she was startled out of a waking reverie or from actual sleep by the sound of more hammering.

Her initial futile chafing at the outrage of her confinement passed surprisingly quickly into resignation as the day wore on. The sun moved across the sky and the light swung around to the far side of the cabin and the shuttered bedroom grew even gloomier. By the time the chinks of daylight that she could see through the boarded-up window had grown dim and faded into night, she'd almost grown accustomed to the constraints of her new empire of blankets in the corner of the room.

After an unknown number of hours, or minutes, she noticed that there was yellow light coming under the bottom of the bedroom door, and she heard Valentine pulling nails. The door swung open.

"I made supper."

Earlier in the day, she'd thought about jumping him the moment he opened the door. She had her crutch with her in the bedroom and she figured that if she removed the straw, the exposed teeth of the rake would make an ugly, effective weapon if they were slammed into a man's face. But somehow the plan had never been implemented, and now Valentine simply stood aside and waited as she climbed out of her nest of blankets, put her weight on the crutch and limped out into the main room.

Instead of following her, Valentine went back into the bedroom and found the chamber pot and brought it out into the main room and stood it over by the door. Christine saw that the door itself had been padlocked. She also saw – and it took her a while to notice because it was already dark outside – that all of the windows had been boarded up.

She was overcome with a real sense of dread. These were not the inconsequential actions of an impetuous man. This was no whim. Valentine was in it for the long haul. She stared at the man she'd married and saw the claw hammer safely tucked into his belt and realized she was in the hands of a competent gaoler.

She found it hard to breathe.

"There's food and there's water. No need to put on no show."

"Valentine, I..."

She thought she was going to faint. She hoped she would, because if there was no other way out of this at least she could escape into unconsciousness, but the very act of hoping brought her back into focus and instead of falling she regained her balance, walked unsteadily to the table and drank some water.

There was venison stew and day-old bread, and nothing sharper for her to eat it with than a spoon. Even though she hadn't eaten all day, she found she had very little appetite but she sat down and ate what she could because she didn't want to waste the opportunity. In an act of deliberate cunning, she also made the meal last as long as she dared because she didn't know exactly what would come next, but she figured that being locked up in the bedroom again had to be a strong possibility. She was afraid that Valentine would pick up on her subterfuge and get mad, but he sat patiently watching her as if he had all the time in the world, and if he noticed that she took thirty seconds just to tear off each tiny mouthful of bread, he didn't seem to be troubled by it.

It was a small victory, but when he made her leave her crutch behind and shut her back in the bedroom again after her meal, it was a victory she savored.

She had no light inside the room, and while she waited for her eyes to adjust, she sat on the edge of the bed. She expected him at any moment to drive the nails home again, but the minutes slipped by and still there was no hammering. It was almost dizzying to know that she could go to the door and work the latch and it would open. The door could not have been left this way by accident, and she clung to the hope that he had after all, in some small way, at last relented.

Nothing happened for a long time, and it seemed as if the situation might continue unchanged if not forever, then at least through the remainder of the night. As Christine sat there tense and upright, peering into the darkness and standing guard over the empty room, she started to feel like a fool. And since it would also have felt faintly absurd to return to the blankets in the corner, when she at last decided to abandon her post, she simply slipped into bed. After a while, she fell asleep.

Some time in the night, she became aware that Valentine had come into the room and was placing something – it must have been the chamber pot – under the bed. She knew immediately on waking that something was terribly wrong. Her first confused thought was that she should be the one coming into the bedroom while Valentine slept, but before she could remember how their roles had come to be reversed, he had thrown back the covers and was already on top of her and then inside her. She didn't fight or call out or speak, and she hung on until it was over by silently reciting the words "I'm being raped" like a mantra, over and over again, around and around until they lost all meaning.

When he was done, Valentine got up and left the room. As soon as he had closed the door behind him, Christine scrambled off of the bed with uncontrollable loathing. She stayed as far away from it as possible and spent the rest of the night on the floor, curled up in the blankets in the corner.

It was already full day outside, but still twilight in the shuttered room when Christine was woken by more hammering outside the bedroom door. She stayed down on the floor wrapped in the security of her blankets and didn't get up to check the door even after Valentine finished his carpentry project and left the cabin for his fields. She left her corner only once that day, to use the chamber pot, and when Valentine opened the door to let her out in the evening, he was obliged to fetch a lantern to light the room so that he could find her and pull her to her feet and take her out into the main room for her supper.

After Christine had eaten and was being led back to her cell, she saw that Valentine, for his greater convenience, had now arranged for the door to be securely fastened with two stout bars rather than having to be nailed shut.

Inside the room she fled immediately to her corner and stayed awake in terror that Valentine would come to her again. Before long he did indeed come into the room, but it was only to replace the chamber pot, and he made no attempt to force himself upon her – neither that night nor any other night for the following week.

At the end of this period, she awoke in the morning to more light than usual and found that the bedroom door was open. She got up from her nest of blankets on the floor and cautiously went out into the main room.

There was no-one there. The whole cabin was empty and quiet. There were still boards nailed up over all of the ground floor windows, but now that she was in the room in day-time, she saw that a high gable-end window had been left uncovered and that light was also coming in through an open vent in the roof.

She also saw that the padlock on the door to the outside had been left unfastened. She went to the door and opened it and left the stuffy cabin and walked outside into the sunshine of a warm summer day.

She went around the side of the house and headed toward the well, and as she went she shed her filthy clothes and dropped them on the ground. The well was twenty yards away, and by the time she reached it she was completely naked. She felt that something was missing and then realized that the silence from inside the cabin had followed her out here; there was no barking from the dogs.

She had no wish to set them off, but since this was the first time they had ever failed to go apeshit at her every coming and going, she was also intensely curious. She approached their run and saw only one dog. It pulled against its chain and looked as menacing as ever, but somehow its growl sounded unconvincing and still it didn't bark. And then beyond the run Christine saw a mound of freshly-turned earth and understood that the dog that had been wounded by the bear and had never completely recovered, must in the end have died.

Although the dogs had scared her and driven her crazy, they were only beasts, and she'd felt no real ill-will toward them. But now she thought of Valentine, and she was glad that one of his dogs had died.

She walked back to the well and worked the hand-pump and tipped bucket after bucket of cold water over her naked body.

The children were surprised to see her when she walked into the school later that morning. But not as surprised as Nathaniel.

"Christine! I think it's fair to say that none of us here

were expecting to see you."

"Cut the crap, Pastor. I need to talk to you."

"Of course. But can't it wait until –"

"OK kids, school's out early today. Come on, let's go."

The children stayed put. They looked to Nathaniel for instructions.

"Christine, I don't understand. Is there some kind of emergency?"

"No, I just thought I'd come all the way down here to piss you off. The foot's a lot better by the way, thanks for asking. It's been getting a lot of rest."

She squeezed herself in at a table where some of the smaller children sat. They stared at her. She waved "hi". Nathaniel shrugged.

"All right, children. I'll see you all tomorrow."

There were no dawdlers. The children usually left the school with quiet, well-behaved efficiency but today they grabbed their things and clattered away down the steps with more haste than Christine had seen before. Perhaps it was just because it was summer, but it almost looked as if they were in awe of her and that they couldn't wait to get away. Christine noticed Ruth and Jessica and nodded to them, but neither one responded. Ruth especially seemed to avoid catching her eye.

When Nathaniel had seen the last child out of the door, he wheeled round to confront her.

"Well?"

"How do I find the Doctor?"

"You didn't have to send everybody home to ask me that."

"The one who helped Ruth. Where does he live?"

"You don't look ill. Not physically. You look quite well in fact."

"I didn't say I was sick, I said I wanted to talk to the Doctor. Will you help me or not?"

"I'm not sure I can."

"Oh for fuck's sake –"

"That's not what I meant. The Doctor's very unwell. Probably dying. Mark didn't come to school today. I think he's with him."

"Well, that sucks for everyone. Except Mark, I suppose."

"Why did you want to see him?"

"Maybe that's none of your business."

"As you wish. You came here for my help. I can't help you if I don't know what you need."

"Then again, maybe it is."

"What does that mean?"

"This is where you thank me for sending home the kids."

"I don't understand you. Does this have something to do with me?"

"I'm pregnant. At least, I think I am."

"You're saying it's mine!?"

"Hardly. Do you people not know how the whole baby thing works?"

"Then it's Valentine's? So this is good news! Or are there complications?"

"He raped me. Twice. And the second time he was very pissed off at you. Do you want to know why, or can you figure it out?"

"What do you want, Christine?"

"I want to get rid of it."

Nathaniel led her to a nearby house that looked as if it was made from a darker wood than most of the other buildings. It must once have been quite elegant too – at least by the community's standards – but over the years its foundations had subsided and now, instead of being merely crooked, the sad remains of its gothic excess made it look exactly like a witch's house from a fairytale.

When the door opened in response to Nathaniel's knocking and Christine saw Miriam, it was so perfect she almost laughed out loud.

"Good day to you, Pastor. But why would you bring with you this grinning baggage?"

"Good day, Miriam. Will you let us in and I'll explain."

"You'll explain first and then we'll see if I shall let you in."

"This woman needs your assistance."

Miriam stepped out of her house and stood very close to Christine, staring in her face as if she were judging the age and soundness of a horse. Without warning, she slipped her ice-cold claw-like hand under Christine's clothes and felt her belly. She seemed satisfied with this exploration and seemed to have arrived at some conclusion, but then she reached her hand further down and before Christine could stop her, she felt her fingers deftly probe the interior of her vagina.

It was over in seconds, and after Miriam stepped away from her again, Christine could not be certain that it had ever happened. But then the old woman sniffed her fingers and licked them, and she made a point of giving Christine an evil, leering grin before she turned to Nathaniel.

"What do you know of this?"

"Only what she has told me."

"You had no hand in it?"

"No hand, nor anything else."

"I do not believe you, but it makes no difference. She is a whore regardless. Come in, both of you."

Miriam walked back into the murky blackness of her house, and Nathaniel and Christine followed. They found the rickety floor of the hall passageway almost impossible to see as they stumbled along behind her and tried to keep up. But the old woman was as swift and sure-footed as a cat.

"In there."

Before scuttling further away down the passageway,

Miriam paused to direct them into a sitting room where the daylight trickled in past the leaves of a massively overgrown bush and then through three thick panes of yellowish glass that looked as though they were melting. The white shapes that hovered in various places around the room turned out to be pieces of lace that had been arranged on the furniture, including – as Christine was amazed to discover – an upright piano. After the violation on the front stoop, she didn't think she was bound by the usual obligations of a house guest, so she went ahead and opened the lid without considering whether their host would have wanted her to or not.

She hardly expected it to be in tune, but she found that none of the keys produced any sound at all, and when she looked inside, she saw that all of the strings had been cut.

The old woman returned, and after she had closed the lid of the piano and replaced the piece of lace on top of it, she turned to Christine.

"You are with child. Not long, about eight weeks. It is a girl. You do not wish to keep it?"

"It's a girl? How do you know that?"

"If you do not want the child to live, then I can help you."

"How? What will you do?"

From somewhere inside her black dress, Miriam produced a bundle of dried herbs.

"Before you go to bed, steep this in boiling water and when it has cooled, drink it down. The taste is bitter, but you must drink it all. The blood will come in the night, and by morning it will be done."

Miriam held out the bundle. Christine hesitated. Nathaniel stepped in and took it and offered it to Christine.

"Take it."

"I don't trust her."

Miriam took back the bundle and hid it in her skirts.

"Then find another way or have your brat."

"Just tell me why you're doing this. I know it's not to help me. You tried to kill me, and you'd still do it if you could."

"My son already has an heir – a boy he will not speak to, born from a worthless woman who was a thousand times your better. He does not need another."

"Your son?! Valentine is your son?!"

"Aye, but you are not my daughter. Be glad that he no longer hears me, for if he did, I'd have him get rid of the both of you. But I will take what I can get – and so should you."

The bundle of herbs was in her hand again, and this time Christine took it.

That evening, Christine and Valentine sat at table together and ate the supper that Christine had prepared. Except for the boards on the windows and the unused bars and padlock, it was almost as if her incarceration had never happened.

"I saw you'd put up a chain across the horses" stalls in the barn."

"That's right."

"I was going to take out one of the horses today, but I couldn't see how to unlock it."

"Your foot's better, ain't it?"

"Pretty much."

"Well then. Ain't nowhere you need to be you need a horse to get you there."

"So what about these boards on the windows? When are you going to take them down?"

"I reckon they can stay up for a while."

"It's summer for fuck's sake."

"You can leave open the door if you want more air."

"I want a divorce."

"Ain't no such thing up here."

"I don't care whether there is or not. I want out. I'm not living here with you any more."

"Right now – and you'll remember how that can change – I'd say you got about as much freedom as a body needs. You do your chores and do as I tell you we wont have no further cause for disagreement."

"That's not how this shit works."

"You ask me, I'd say that's exactly how it works."

After supper, Valentine showed no inclination to go to bed. Christine waited to see what would happen – she had no desire to return to the bedroom voluntarily, and in any case she had no idea of what their sleeping arrangements were going to be from now on – and before too long, without a word of goodnight, he went out of the cabin and she heard him padlock the door from the outside.

It was small comfort to know that her new prison was larger and furnished with a lantern, but at least she was now being treated better than the horses.

She took out the bundle of herbs that Miriam had given her and thought about brewing the concoction there and then, but although she was still determined to get rid of the child – a girl, as she couldn't help remembering – she was also feeling too unsettled. In the end, since there was no urgency to act immediately, she decided she could just as well do it tomorrow as today.

She could have made up a place to sleep out in the main room of the cabin, but it seemed important to reclaim the bedroom, so she took the lantern and, leaving the door open behind her, she went inside. She realized that sleeping on the bed itself was an absolute impossibility, and she set about straightening the pile of covers that were still lying on the floor in the corner of the room. Then she blew out the lantern and lay down, and with the bed squatting a few feet away from her like some loathsome reptile, almost more repellent than Valentine himself, she went to sleep.

She awoke early the next day and found that the cabin door had already been opened and that as before, she had been left free to come and go as she pleased.

She prepared and ate her breakfast, and after that she washed pots and cleaned the kitchen and swabbed the cabin floor. She had a strange urge to clean the windows, but it would have been frustrating and pointless as long as there were still boards nailed up over them outside.

She wandered out to the barn, not so much to check that the horses had been fed – which was not a task that Valentine was likely to forget – but really just to visit them. It wasn't the chains across their stalls that made her feel sad, but the fact that they were in their separate stalls at all. At this time of year, horses belonged outside, grazing together in a summer meadow.

She went listlessly from the barn to the well and from there to the vegetable garden. She even went to look at the surviving dog. She orbited the cabin. Was this going to be her life from now on, forever and ever? Moving in smaller and smaller circles as the seasons rolled around, growing older until she found herself nodding by an unlit stove, waiting to be warmed by the crackle of a dead radio and without so much as a living cat to keep her company?

Such a life would be tolerable, but it would also be insane. How did people do it? Was there some trick that you could learn – a trick more subtle and more powerful than any opiate or alkaloid – that would turn off part of your brain? Was she already in danger of learning it? Or would it be her salvation? She thought of the people of the community and what she had seen of how they lived. Since their ancestors had settled here in this remote unwanted corner of the earth, the outside world had had a hundred birthdays and they'd missed every one.

And all the time her mind kept coming back to the life that was growing inside her. Perhaps a child could have been the answer – the one thing that would give her life meaning and purpose – but it was too late now, because by the next morning that life would be gone.

"Miss Christine."

It was the hushed voice of a young woman, or a girl, and it seemed to come from somewhere impossibly close.

Christine glimpsed movement in a patch of grassy weeds and bushes that marked the edge of the forest. Then the foliage parted and she saw a face and a beckoning arm.

"Ruth? Is that you?"

"Please. No one must know I'm here."

Christine played her part and did what she could to allay the girl's melodramatic fears, but she still felt faintly ridiculous as she crawled on her hands and knees into the middle of the patch of weeds. Like Ruth, she hoped that no-one would see them, but for a different reason.

"It's good to see you. Really. But what's this all about?"

"I'm so sorry about what happened. I didn't know he'd be so mad."

"Who?"

"Mr Woods."

"You mean Valentine? Ruth, what did you do?"

"It was me that told on you. About being with the Pastor. I meant you harm –"

"God almighty, Ruth, why would you do something like that? What have I ever done to hurt you?"

"I'm sorry. I shouldn't have done it. I wish I hadn't."

"Fucking A. What is wrong with you?"

"Miss Christine, I've come here to warn you."

"Yeah, well you're about a week too late."

"No, I mean – You went to see Miss Miriam."

"Great. So everyone knows about that too?"

"She gave you something. Something bad. A poison. You mustn't take it."

"Ruth, I don't know how much they've told you about these things, but it's a special kind of poison."

"Yes, I know. It's to kill the baby. But it'll do more than that. You mustn't take it."

"Well, I haven't taken it. Not yet."

"I know – of course you haven't, else you'd be dead."

"How do you know all this?"

"Everyone knows. Everyone except Mr Woods."

"Look, I don't trust the old witch myself, but you're telling me everyone knows she's trying to kill me and nobody says a thing?"

"I'm saying it."

"Yeah, but only you? Nobody else? Pastor Nathaniel was right there. You don't think he would have said something?"

"She tried to kill you before. You think she hates you any less now than she did then?"

"Probably not, but she was kinda flipped out at the time. You really think she'd murder me in cold blood? And that everyone in the community would just let her? I mean, wow."

"You're an outsider. No-one will care if you die. Except me."

The girl looked away. Christine thought she was going to cry. She wasn't good in these situations and she wasn't sure what to do, so she took the girl's hand in her own.

"Look, Ruth, I really appreciate you coming out here to tell me all this. And I forgive you for telling Valentine about the Pastor, so don't sweat it, OK? If you want to know, our marriage was already pretty much fucked, so no real harm done."

"You won't take it, will you?"

"The witch's poison? Well, you can bet I'm going to think twice about it now."

It wasn't much of a promise, but Ruth seemed satisfied with it. She nodded and wiped her eyes and started to creep away toward the woods. Still keeping her voice low, Christine called after her:

"And that thing you have for the Pastor. It's OK you know. I know what it's like and it's not always easy, but there's nothing wrong with you. The jealousy's a bitch and there's not much I can say to help you deal with it, but even that will pass. Hang in there, kid. You'll get through it. Everything's going to be OK."

Christine found it hard to take the threat seriously. She had no doubt that Ruth's warning was well-meant and sincere, and it certainly made sense that the old woman – Valentine's mother! – would want her dead, but it was another thing again to believe that she'd calmly go about actually doing it. Even so, Christine thought it would do no harm to leave things as they were for at least one more day, and that night she once again went to her pile of blankets on the floor without drinking Miriam's concoction.

All this talk of death and murder also revived Christine's interest in her husband's previous wife – and especially the question of how she had died. Although the witch made no secret of her hatred for Valentine's first bride, if she had poisoned her too, then everyone would know about it and Ruth would have used it as part of her argument. So it seemed unlikely that the late Mrs Woods had died from poisoning. But if not by poison, then how?

Christine was inclined to think that she must have died in childbirth. That would neatly account for Valentine's rejection of his son, and also his reluctance to talk about it. Perhaps he felt guilty. Perhaps the bastard even still loved her. Perhaps the locked room was a shrine to her memory.

Christine didn't know, but it suddenly felt very important to find out.

She slept badly that night, and she was still groggy at breakfast. Even Valentine noticed it.

"You still sleeping on the floor?"

"I prefer it."

"Don't make much sense. It's a perfectly good bed in there."

"It's a perfectly good floor too."

"I could use a bed."

"It's your bed. Help yourself."

"Then I'll take it out into the barn."

"Knock yourself out."

"I'll see to it presently. You strip it down and be sure it's all set to move."

After breakfast, Christine went into the bedroom, and after glaring at the hated bed for a moment, she started to strip it down. She tore off the rest of the covers and tossed the bolsters out into the main room. When she tried to roll up the stained, heavy, lumpy, feather mattress, she only managed to more or less fold it in half, but she figured Valentine could take it from there. And fuck it, he could take care of the massive frame too because she had no idea how that was supposed to come apart. She took another look to see if she was missing anything obvious, and then she saw a part of the wall that had until then been hidden by the bed's headboard. Or rather, she saw a hole where the wall should have been.

It wasn't that much of a hole. It was only a foot wide — the width of the broken board — and it ran up a couple of feet from the floor and left some of the framing lumber exposed.

But although the boards on the other side were all intact and Christine couldn't see all the way through to the next room, she was pretty sure that just beyond the wall was the room that was always kept locked. And now she knew how she was going to get into the junk room where Valentine kept his first wife's purple dress.

Later that morning, when Christine was busy scrubbing root vegetables out by the well, she watched Valentine out of the corner of her eye as he came tramping up from the lower fields where he'd been toiling. She watched him go into the cabin and then come out again half a minute later. As she waited for him to speak, she tried to gauge his mood, which was never easy because he wore the same expression – his inscrutable "cowboy face" – pretty much the whole time.

"I said to get the bed stripped down and now you got it all made up again."

"I changed my mind."

"That's not what you said before."

"Well, no, because that's kind of the whole point about changing your mind. Look, Valentine, I thought about it and you were right: it's dumb to keep sleeping on the floor."

"So now I come all the way up here for no reason."

"Yeah, I tried to call you, but I guess you forgot to take your phone."

"Don't need no phone if you stick to what you say you'll do."

"At least now you don't have to move it."

He thought about that for a moment as he stood watching her clean the vegetables. Was he suspicious, or was he just thinking about how he'd be sleeping out in the barn without a bed after all? Or maybe he was making up his mind to take the bed anyway?

"Are those for supper?"

He helped himself to a carrot and took a bite and munched on it absently as he headed back to the fields.

Once Valentine had left the cabin in the morning, he usually stayed out for the whole day, but now that his routine had already been disrupted, Christine judged it too risky to start working on the wall right away. The most she dared do was search around in the barn and try to figure out what tools were kept out there that she might be able to use.

She also knew that even if Valentine no longer seemed likely to come to her in the hours of darkness, he sometimes came to check on her before she was up, and if he found her still sleeping on the floor after all the shit she'd just put him through, she didn't think she could talk her way past him a second time. So from now on she'd have to sleep in the bed again all through the night – and she wasn't sure if she could handle it. All through the long summer day, the prospect loomed over her like a nightmare, hideous and inevitable, and coming closer and closer as the sun moved across the sky and the shadows lengthened. In just a few more hours she'd be lowering herself into a hateful, stinking pit of noxious fluids and excrement.

With so much else to deal with, there was no question of drinking Miriam's fatal tea, and her intended abortion was once again put on hold.

She rose at sun-up and immediately left the bed and refused to acknowledge anything at all about the night she had just spent in the place where she had been violated. Once she was safely out in the cabin's main room, the memory erased itself of its own accord and allowed her to think of herself as clean again.

The cabin was empty and Valentine was almost certainly working in the fields by now, but just to make sure that he was gone, she dawdled over breakfast and then forced herself to wait for at least another hour. She was afraid to screw things up from undue haste and she was afraid to find out that her plan wouldn't work and she was also just afraid, period.

She went outside and looked down toward the fields to see if she could catch sight of Valentine and be certain where he was. As usual he was nowhere to be seen, but as there could be no certainty anyway, she went ahead and walked out to the barn.

By this time she almost took it as a matter of course that everything she did was spied upon, so on her way back to the cabin with her arms full of an awkward assortment of tools, she did her best to stroll along as casually as possible. She felt so cunning and clever and ridiculous that it was all she could do to stop herself from ostentatiously whistling an innocent tune.

In the bedroom she set up the lantern and wondered about closing the door while she worked, but decided that it would be better to leave it open so that at least she'd have a chance of hearing Valentine come into the cabin if for some reason he returned home early. The feather mattress alone was heavy enough and the bed as a whole was too massive to move, so to gain access to the wall behind the headboard, she hauled up the mattress from the top half of the bed and then removed the supporting boards that were underneath it. With the boards gone, she could now see the floor beneath the bed – and also the chamber pot, which she took out and moved out of the way to the side of the room.

Her plan was simply to kick out the boards on the other side of the wall until the hole was big enough for her to squeeze through, but she didn't know how long it would take. She knew that she couldn't stop Valentine from finding out eventually, but she meant to keep it from him for as long as possible – at least long enough for her to properly explore the room, and hopefully not until she'd figured out some way to leave the bastard altogether. She also knew that Valentine was an observant son-of-a-bitch who'd notice any frontal assault on the junk room's boarded-up window or the locked door itself the moment he came home.

But Christine's more devious approach had its downside too. For one thing, it was a bitch to work in the confined space under the headboard while standing inside the bed-frame. She'd hoped to force her way through by hitting the back of the other wall as hard as she could, but she found it almost impossible to get a good clean swing and strike a decent blow and none of the tools were well-suited to the purpose. She had a little more luck with a pry-bar, but progress was frustratingly slow and after several hours all she'd managed to do was loosen some of the boards: she could push them an inch or so out of place so that her lantern lit up a small strip of floor in the other room, but as soon as she let go, they'd snap back again.

Another problem was that at the end of each day's work – and although it couldn't have been any later than mid-afternoon, she thought it wise to finish up earlier rather than later – she had to put the bed back together again and straighten everything up. When she came to replace the boards in the bed frame, she discovered that each board needed to be slotted into its own particular place, and solving this puzzle by the light of a lantern was by no means easy. This task alone took much longer than she'd expected and she was glad she'd left a generous margin. She'd originally meant to take the tools back out to the barn again, but it was now growing so late that she thought it safer just to leave them under the bed.

Most frustrating of all was the thought of how little progress she'd made. A whole day and she'd gotten almost nowhere – and the longer it took, the more chance Valentine would have of catching her. She needed to figure out how to speed things up.

The next day she awoke to find Valentine staring at her from the bedroom doorway. He looked like he had something he wanted to say, but after a few moments he turned and left without a word. She hoped he hadn't spotted anything amiss, and she was glad that the torment she'd suffered by sleeping in the hateful bed had at least not been endured for nothing.

As before, she waited until she was reasonably sure that Valentine had left the cabin for the day, but this time, after she'd peeled back the mattress and removed the boards and carefully stacked them in order, she set to work on the framing lumber with an ancient saw that was in desperate need of sharpening. The angle was awkward and although she did what she could to create some clearance, she was only able to make short strokes.

She sawed until her hands hurt, and then she wrapped a rag around her blistered palm and sawed some more. She wanted to rest but she forced herself to keep going until the frame was almost cut through. For the last half-inch of wood, she lay down and stomped on it with her heel. At the third try, her efforts were finally rewarded: the frame split with a satisfying wrench and several of the wall-boards in the junk room now dangled so freely that you could move them with one finger.

The hole – really it was more like a cat flap – was now definitely big enough, but much as she wanted to crawl through right away, it was time to clean up and re-assemble the bed. She noticed that now that the frame inside the wall had failed, some cracks had also opened up in the wall above the bed, but they were hard to see with the lantern and even harder to see without it. She decided to leave it be and hope for the best. Besides, there wasn't much that she could do about it.

At supper, Valentine noticed how Christine favored her injured hand. He grabbed her wrist and saw the blisters on her palm.

"What? I burned it."

"Is that right?"

"Yes it is. And it hurts like fuck."

"You should be more careful."

The next morning, Christine awoke with the over-whelming conviction that Valentine had never for a moment believed that she'd burned her hand, and it drove her crazy not to know why he hadn't called her on it. Did he just not care about her injury or her lie? Or did he already know everything and just wanted to see how far she'd go before he pounced?

Well, screw Valentine. Today she was going through that wall. After all, if he already knew everything, she had nothing to lose.

There was no sense in being reckless though, so as well as giving him plenty of time to get clear of the cabin and head out to the fields, this morning she took the extra precaution of sneaking a few hundred yards through the woods to where she could actually see him at work. And sure enough, there he was walking behind a single-blade plow pulled by two of the horses, turning a long strip of oats stubble back into the soil.

Thirty minutes later, she was reaching through the hole in the wall to place the lantern on the junk room floor, and a moment after that she was pushing the boards aside and crawl-ing through after it.

She felt like she'd arrived in one of those "country an-tique" stores that can always be found along the main street of every small American town. The kind of place that be-gins as a yard sale and then moves permanently indoors as the owner/proprietor gets tired of moving the heavy cabinets and wobbly tables and lurching shelves back and forth each day, after which curiosities of all sorts – painted metal trains, inlaid wooden boxes, colored pebbles that resemble the eggs of songbirds – start to accumulate on top of the larger pieces of furniture and lumber, until twenty or sixty or a hundred years later, the whole worthless sagging undusted heap has acquired a character and archeology all of its own.

Christine was disappointed to discover that the room seemed to hold almost nothing of any real value. The drawers that she'd hoped to ransack – all of which were twisted and swollen and hard to open – were empty except for a few coins and the front page of a Spanish-language newspaper that had been used for lining and which reported on the 1896 Cinquo del Mayo festivities in Monterrey.

Even the abandoned toys, which might have shed some light on Valentine's childhood, and perhaps even his boyhood personality – Christine wondered if he'd ever seen a real train – were of little interest to her now that she felt nothing but hatred for the man who had once played with them.

The most recent additions to the room were the two objects that Christine had previously mistaken for birdcages. She saw now that they were wire frame mannequins designed to emulate the shape of a human torso – tailor's dummies, one male and one female, which could be adjusted to match the exact dimensions of the person being modeled. The male frame was a good fit to Valentine, and if the female frame was equally accurate, his first wife must have been trim and well-proportioned – very much of Christine's build in fact, which would explain why the purple dress had fitted her so well.

But where was the dress itself? There was no doubt that Valentine had fetched it from this room and afterward returned it here too. She raised the lantern higher – and saw that what she had at first taken to be a wall at the far end of the room was in fact a folding wooden screen.

There was something vaguely private and forbidding about the screen. It was as if her disdainful wandering through the rambling public spaces of an antique store owned by a superficially friendly young man – who nevertheless somehow felt not quite right – had somehow led her to be standing on the threshold of his actual living quarters.

The opportunity was there, but did she really want to see what lay beyond? She tried to remember why she had come so far, and almost thought of turning back.

She pulled the screen aside – and found not only the dress, but also the dressmaker.

The remains of Valentine's first wife were manacled to the wall. Her unburied body sat slumped on the floor in a soiled linen petticoat, and there were shreds of shriveled leathery skin stretched over the yellowed bones of her skull. Her hair was the same color as Christine's.

The purple dress had been tossed across a nearby vanity and lay next to a small, neat pile of other clothes, all of which were carefully folded and, in the absence of any tissue paper, loosely wrapped in pages taken from the same Mexican newspaper that had been used to line the drawer.

The vanity also had a mirror – the first that Christine had seen since since she'd left Tulum – and now in the mirror she saw movement behind her.

"I see that you and Emily been getting acquainted."

Valentine had her cornered. He'd come back to the cabin and silently unlocked the door and now he was standing in the doorway and there was no hope of getting past him.

"You womenfolk are all the same. Ain't a one of you a man can trust. And you can string together whatever words you like, it won't matter none because I know it ain't my child."

"It is!"

"You believe it if you want, but I know all about it. The child she bore was the Pastor's son."

Christine didn't know if it was true or not, but she saw how far his paranoia was out of control and it sent a chill through her bones. Valentine was completely unhinged – and he was blocking the room's only doorway.

But she wasn't about to give up without a fight. She charged across the room and threw herself at the damaged wall.

With the frame already broken, a large section of wall split apart and as more boards tore loose from the ceiling, she burst through the wall and crashed into the bedroom on the other side.

She found herself sprawling on the floor by the bed. The open bedroom door was right in front of her. She scrambled to her feet and her heart leaped with the thought that after all she'd gotten away from him – but somehow Valentine tackled her from behind and now he was on top of her and she was hitting him but it made no difference and he caught hold of her lower arm and while she kicked and tried to gouge his eyes with her free hand, he fastened a manacle about her other wrist and chained her to the frame of the bed.

"I seen the chamber pot where you left it by the window and when I looked and saw tools missing from the barn, I knew you was fixing to go in there but I couldn't hardly believe it after what I told you. I said you weren't to go in there, and now you went and did it."

Christine was sobbing.

"You bastard, let me go."

"Can't let you go when you can't be trusted."

"You're sick, Valentine. Really. There's something wrong with you. Just let me go and you'll never see me again I swear.

"How could I never see you again? What you're swearing to ain't possible."

He left her there, chained to the bed, defeated and in

despair. And now that most of the wall had been destroyed, if she looked beyond the derelict furniture and tailor's dummies, lit by the light of the lantern that she'd left behind, she could see Emily's sagging corpse still sitting on the floor.

All through the rest of the summer, he kept her chained up like a dog. The week-long confinement to her room had been bad but this was far worse. She no longer even had the illusion of freedom – this time there were no more evenings when she'd sit with Valentine at supper and the door of the cabin would be right there for her to walk through, at least in her imagination. This time she was kept chained up to some post or rafter from morning to evening as she did her chores, and then chained to the bed again all through the night. The weight of the manacle on her wrist was always there, and the door of the cabin no longer had any meaning.

There was also the problem of her pregnancy, which she tried to hide but which inevitably was becoming more and more noticeable. Christine didn't know what evidence – if any – Valentine might have had for thinking Mark was the Pastor's son, but since everyone in the community apparently knew about her affair with Nathaniel, even a perfectly sane man might reasonably wonder whose child she was carrying. To a man as unstable as Valentine, even the mathematical certainty that the child was his would be no guarantee that he wouldn't chain her to the wall next to Emily, seal up the room again and leave her to rot.

She still had the herbs that Miriam had given her, and at first she'd thought of drinking the infusion despite Ruth's warning. But now, instead of fearing death, she was more afraid that the potion would work: if the baby miscarried – and if she could dispose of the fetus in the outhouse before Valentine saw it – then her reward would be to live as a slave in chains for the rest of her life.

It would be better just to die, either by the potion or by some other method – and that's what she would have done except that it would mean she'd now be killing the baby for no reason. What she really wanted was to kill herself but not the baby. And whatever happened, the only way she could achieve that was to carry the child to full term and wait for it to be born – which was something that Valentine would never allow.

Her situation was impossible – and she could see only one way out. Hour after hour, as she blindly went about her chores, in her head she ran through the same arguments over and over again, and each time she reached the same inevitable conclusion. Valentine had to die. She had to poison him.

The idea was simple enough, and she was more than willing to do it. By now she wanted him dead more than she wanted anything. But although her conscience was clear – it was her life or his, and there was no doubt that he deserved it – still, the act itself was terrifying, and she always found a reason to postpone the attempt for one more day. She also knew that there could be no second chance, and always, in the back of her mind, there was one even more terrifying thought: What if she tried and failed?

And then one oppressive summer morning, after Valentine had shackled her chain to the rafters in the kitchen before he went out to the fields or rode off hunting or wherever the fuck it was he was going, instead of just leaving, he paused and stared at her.

"You look different."

"You keep me chained up for two months and you expect me to look the same?"

"Better than before."

"Yeah? Then I guess it's a shame you didn't chain me up sooner."

"Heavier too."

"You wanna know my secret?"

"What secret?"

"Lots of potatoes and no exercise. That'll do it every time."

She turned away from him and started to clear up the breakfast things. She felt the weight of his eyes on her back, and tried to make her ass sag. This conversation had to be shut down, but it was beyond her control and all she could do was silently will him to leave. After what seemed like forever, he finally stopped watching her and went out the door without another word.

When she was sure that he had really gone, she counted to twenty just to make sure and only then allowed herself to slump against the table with a sigh of relief. Physically, it was true that she felt good. Despite everything she was in suspiciously good shape. It must be the hormones kicking in.

In any case, one thing was clear: she dared not delay any longer.

Around the middle of the afternoon, she fished out the package of Miriam's herbs from the bodice of the shapeless dress that she wore every day. It was smaller than she remembered, and it was crumpled and squashed from being carried around for so long. After so much time, the leaves had become dry and brittle, and the bundle as a whole looked absurdly harmless. Christine began to doubt if it would have any effect on Valentine at all. Nevertheless, she treated it with the greatest respect as she transferred every last sprig from the cloth pouch to a bowl and painstakingly ground the leaves into a powder.

There was one more hurdle to overcome: the taste. From Miriam's original instructions, Christine had formed the impression that the herbs would be exceedingly bitter. It seemed unlikely that Valentine would have a refined or sensitive palate, but he'd already sensed that something was wrong, and if he ever thought that she was trying to poison him...

She wet her fingertip and dipped it into the powder and licked the smudge of powder off her finger. It was no more bitter than dust, and except for a slight metallic aftertaste that might only have been her imagination, it tasted of nothing at all. A few moments after she'd swallowed the powder, she felt a painful twinge in her abdomen. But she'd felt similar twinges before and when nothing further happened, she put it down to coincidence.

Satisfied that the potion would be undetectable, she put the bowl aside. Then, using the kitchen knife that Valentine had chained to the sink, she diced deer meat and root vegetables into a pot, added water and put the pot on to simmer. She'd made the exact same stew every night for as long as she could remember. It was the last thing she wanted to eat on a warm summer evening, but Valentine never complained, and she wasn't about to get experimental. Besides, venison was almost ideally suited to her purpose: it had a strong flavor which would help to conceal any remaining bitterness.

An hour or so before she expected Valentine to return for his dinner, she added a spoonful of liquid from the stew to the powdered herbs in the bowl and mixed them into a paste. Everything was set. She wondered if she should check the flavor again, but decided not to. All she had to do now was fret and wait until Valentine came home so that she could serve the bastard his final supper.

It was past sundown when she at last heard his footsteps outside the cabin. She'd almost thought that he'd gone out on one of his extended hunting trips, or that he'd maybe had some fatal accident — on this day of all days — and wouldn't be coming home any more at all. But now here he was, entering without a word and pulling off his boots and sitting at the table and ignoring her so completely and effortlessly that she wondered if he actually knew that she was there. He was so impassive she found it hard to believe that he was even human. Christine found herself staring at him as if he were an object — as if he were some soulless phantom made solid, a ghost who'd drifted into this world of men and women by mistake, and who needed to be dissolved again by the magic of her potion.

She placed a glass of water on the table in front of him. He drank it unquestioningly. Christine told herself that everything was going to be all right.

She ladled a portion of stew into the bowl with the paste of herbs and another portion into a clean bowl and brought them both to the table. He stared at the food in confusion.

"What's this?"

Spoons! She'd forgotten the spoons. Her mouth had fallen open, so she closed it and got up hastily and grabbed a couple of spoons and gave him one. Should she say something, make some wise-ass remark? That's what she always did, right? About the crazy day she'd had and how there was so much going on in her life that she could hardly be expected to remember every tiny detail. Would it be suspicious if she stayed silent —

Valentine was already eating.

But did he always look like that? Was that the expression he always wore when he was shoveling stew into his mouth? It suddenly occurred to her that if the herbs were meant to be drunk as an infusion, then perhaps being steeped in hot liquid would bring out their bitterness? But it was too late now. She was committed. Either she was about to be busted or her husband was about to be poisoned. She resigned herself to whichever outcome with a shrug.

"Fuck it."

Valentine did no more than glance at her and then went back to finishing the stew. When he was done, he pushed his empty bowl toward her.

"You want more, you can have mine. I'm not hungry."

"You're always hungry."

"So, what? Now you're suspicious?"

"Suspicious of what?"

"You're such a fucking idiot."

As if reassured by her impotent obscenity, he ignored her, took her bowl and started eating. Halfway through he started to slow down. Another minute and he was pausing to take a breath between mouthfuls. Shortly after that he was writhing on the floor clutching his stomach.

Christine got up and went over to him. She took a length of the chain that fastened her manacle to the kitchen rafter and looped it around his neck. He struggled and she pulled it tighter. If he preferred to be strangled to death, that was fine with her.

His elbow suddenly hit her hard in the face, and as she fell backward, before the pain kicked in, all she felt was an enormous sense of relief that he hadn't punched her in the stomach.

But her nose hurt like hell and she could taste blood and she could hardly see and when she touched her hand to her face it came away smeared with red and the pain in her nose was indescribable. And Valentine had somehow crawled away and was now curled up and groaning in a heap over by the door.

She blinked and wiped her eyes and gazed at what would have happened to her if she'd trusted Miriam — or if Ruth hadn't come to warn her about the witch's true intention.

Christine watched as Valentine lost all control of his muscles. He convulsed a couple of times and passed out. There was brown drool running from his mouth and judging from the smell, he'd soiled himself.

"Don't die on me now, you bastard, not all the way over there!"

Her desperate cry had no effect. Valentine remained

where he was, sprawled unconscious on the floor a good ten feet beyond the extremity of her chain with the key to her manacle in his pocket. There was no way she could reach him or drag him closer. If he was as dead as he seemed to be, then she'd eventually die here with him – and if he somehow recovered, then no doubt he'd make sure that she died even sooner.

There was nothing more that she could do, and now that it was over she felt strangely detached. She expected at any moment to be crushed beneath an avalanche of despair or racked by uncontrollable sobs of rage and frustration at the sheer bloody-mindedness of how things had turned out, but while she waited for these emotions to sweep over her – and for the pain behind her nose to subside – she found herself sitting back down at the table and wondering if this counted as victory.

Of course, it wasn't exactly the outcome she'd hoped for, but after all, her plan had mostly worked and she was hardly any worse off than before. Plus she'd made the bastard suffer, she was sure of that. If she felt anything at all, it was a sense of quiet satisfaction. She also realized that she was actually quite hungry, and remembered that she'd had almost nothing to eat all day. She retrieved her bowl from the floor, filled it with untainted stew and calmly ate her supper.

The cabin door opened and early morning sunlight streamed into the room.

Christine raised her groggy head from the kitchen table where she'd spent the whole night. She squinted at the figure of a girl silhouetted in the doorway.

"Ruth?"

"What happened to Mr Woods?"

"You were right about those herbs that Miriam gave me."

"Is he dead?"

Ruth came further into the room. She skirted around the body, peering at it from several feet away.

"Ruth, listen: he has a key in one of his pockets. Can you get it for me?"

Ruth shook her head.

"I don't want to touch him."

"It's OK. He's not going to hurt you."

"It's not that. He smells bad."

"Yeah, I think he shit himself."

"Don't you smell it?"

"I must have gotten used to it – Look, I really need you to do this. I'm going to be here forever unless you can find that key. It'll be OK. Just don't get too close to his butt."

Ruth reached into the breast pocket of Valentine's shirt. Nothing.

"OK, you need to check his pants. Just pat him down from outside. It's a big key. You should feel it if it's there."

Ruth ran her hand over the thick material of Valentine's work-pants.

"Anything?"

"Yeah, but I don't think it's a key."

"Ruth, believe me, I'm sorry, but you have to make sure."

Ruth thought for a moment, then moved around the body to get a better angle. She slipped her hand into Valentine's front pants pocket and worked her way deeper and deeper inside. Her probing fingers touched something. She grabbed it, pulled it out, backed away from the body with a shudder, and brought it to Christine. It was a small clasp-knife.

"Shit."

"Christine?"

"Yeah?"

"He's still warm."

"Christ."

There was a brief silence as they both absorbed the idea

that Valentine might, after all, still be alive. Christine stared at the body. If it had been within her power – and within her reach – she would have stabbed it in the neck with the clasp knife. She thought about asking Ruth to do it for her, but even if her husband really was now nothing more than a corpse, it still seemed like too big a favor to ask a fourteen-year-old girl.

"Isn't it possible. . . ? I mean, it was a warm night."

"How long has he been lying there?"

"Since a little after sundown."

"If he died at sundown, he should be cold by now."

"Are you sure? What if he didn't die right away?"

"Christine?"

"Yeah?"

"What happens when he wakes up?"

"When he wakes up, we both need to be gone. He still has one more pocket. You need to roll him over."

This time there was no squeamishness or hesitation. Finding the key was now just an unpleasant task that needed to be done as quickly and efficiently as possible. Ruth grabbed hold of Valentine's shoulder and hauled him over onto his back. She thrust her hand into the other front pocket of his pants and rummaged around – and still found nothing.

It didn't make any sense. The key definitely existed, so why couldn't they find it? Christine thought furiously.

"OK, if it's not on him, then he must have hidden it somewhere outside because a lot of times when he moved me from one room to another, he'd step out for a moment."

Ruth was already outside, checking in all the likely places.

Inside, Christine could do no more than pace helplessly and call out unnecessary advice:

"It's probably somewhere obvious, and it's got to be nearby..."

The sounds of Ruth scrabbling around outside the door moved further away, and then from beyond the cabin there was only silence. Christine also fell silent. She knew unmistak-ably that Ruth had gone, and although the girl must have had good reason and would surely return at any moment, Christine was at last, abruptly, plunged into despair.

When Ruth came back several minutes later with a large hammer and a metal spike that she'd found in the barn, Christine was once again slumped at the kitchen table, but this time she was crying softly. Both of her eyes were red, and one of them was half-closed and swollen black and purple and yellow where Valentine had struck her in the face. She looked at the girl blankly.

"There's no key, but I found this."

They chose a link in the chain that was slightly twisted and about a foot away from the manacle itself and laid it across a corner of the kitchen table and pinned it there with the spike. Christine had to rest her manacled hand on the table, and since the hammer needed two hands and room to swing, it fell to Ruth to pound the spike. Although there was no danger of accidentally hitting the manacle, and Christine had already pad-ded it with rags, every blow wrenched the chain and jerked the metal bracelet so that it tore at the tender flesh of her wrist.

But it was working. Ruth had already burst the weld that held the link together, and now she drove the spike deep into the wood of the table, forcing the two ends of the loop of iron further and further apart.

And then, beneath the steady, regular crash of metal on metal and the creak of splintering wood, they became aware of another sound, a long, rattling groan that somehow continued endlessly without ever pausing to draw breath. Ruth stopped hammering and they both looked at the body lying on its back by the door. The sound was coming from his stomach, and for the moment, Valentine still seemed to be unconscious, but there was no longer any doubt that he'd survived after all. And they both knew that if he woke – when he woke – they'd want to be as far away as possible.

It all depended on Ruth — and of all the people in the community, there could hardly have been a better choice. Christine almost hugged her for the way she calmly went back to hammering on the spike without a word needing to be said.

Half a dozen more methodical blows from Ruth and the spike finally split the table-leg and the whole wrecked table tipped over and smashed to the floor. But the link had parted. The chain was broken.

Christine was free.

CHAPTER 12

"He's waking up."

Sure enough, Valentine was moving one of his arms. Not very effectively – he'd raise it a few inches and then it would flop back down again – but he was evidently on the threshold of consciousness and already he seemed to be trying to roll over onto his side.

Christine looked at the massive hammer in Ruth's hands. She even picked up the metal spike that had fallen to the floor when the link broke... But then she threw it down again.

"Come on. Don't let him see that it's you."

They dodged around Valentine, whose arms were flailing now, although he was still apparently sightless, or at least very poorly coordinated. As they plunged out into the sunshine they heard a bellow of rage behind them and then another crash.

They ran to the barn where the horses were kept. Christine unbarred the door and for a moment the two of them just stood there looking at each other. Then Christine took the girl in her arms and hugged her as she'd wanted to do two minutes earlier, or possibly forever. Ruth let herself be held for only a short while before she gently pulled away. Without a word, she squeezed Christine's hand, smiled an ambiguous smile and then she slipped away into the woods and was gone.

Christine hurried into the barn. Valentine kept all five

of his horses in a single large stall, and a sense of trouble had spread among them like a contagion. But their restlessness was calmed by her presence. She moved between them swiftly and decisively, and saddled up her favorite mare without too much difficulty.

Before she led the mare out of the stall, she took another twenty seconds to throw open the stall door and drive the other horses outside. She'd expected them to bolt, but when she came back out of the barn and hastily mounted up, she found that not only was Valentine already stumbling out of the cabin toward her, but the liberated horses had gone no further than a sunlit patch of meadow, where they whickered and pranced contentedly as they cantered back and forth.

Valentine was still barely able to walk, and she was in no immediate danger of being caught, especially now that she was on horseback. But she figured she only had a few minutes before he recovered well enough to ride, and even in the open he could probably catch one of the loose horses easily enough, so she rode at them hard, intending to drive them further away. Instead of fleeing, the horses merely scattered – but then they regrouped and circled around and fell in behind her, and when she plunged ahead into the forest, all four of Valentine's other horses continued to lope along after her.

After twenty minutes of easy riding, she slowed the pace to a trot. The whole business with the horses had gone better than she could have hoped for, and together with the success of the witch's potion and her almost miraculous escape – not to mention the relief of not having committed murder after all – she now found herself at the head of a string of magnificent horses heading north through the dappled light of the forest with the whole summer's day ahead of her. Her biggest immediate problem was to keep a grip on her elation in case it tipped over into hysteria.

Still, she had no doubt that Valentine would make every

effort to hunt her down. She'd thought about trying to confuse any possible pursuit by deliberately setting off in the wrong direction, but Valentine's woodcraft was certainly greater than hers, and it seemed unlikely that he'd ever be fooled by such a transparent ruse. For the same reason, she made no attempt to conceal her tracks. After all, they both knew where she was headed: she had no clear idea of how she was going to cross the desert – apart from anything else, she didn't even have a canteen – but if she could only reach it, then civilization was just a few days away on the other side. And while the forest was Valentine's second home, even he might think twice before pursuing her across such hostile terrain.

Meanwhile at least she had a head start, and taking everything into account, she figured her best chance was simply to get as far away from the community as fast as possible. From her climb to the lookout point, she knew more or less where the desert lay, and although almost all of her hunting trips with Valentine had been in the opposite direction, she was able to work her way steadily north by following the contours of the massive range of mountains to the west.

She pushed the mare fairly hard, and for hour after hour, with only short breaks for watering at some of the lively forest streams that were fed by snowmelt from the mountains, the animal continued to respond well. The loose horses also stayed with them and kept pace without any problem. But by early evening, as the sun swung to the north of due west and dipped below the peaks of the range, she began to wonder how and where she might best make camp for the short summer night. Her main concern was how to corral the extra horses. She had no rope or spare bridles, and she was afraid that unless she somehow hitched them to a tree or at least hobbled them, they would wander away and then turn instinctively homeward – straight back to Valentine, who would immediately make good use of them to ride after her.

Of course he might already have borrowed a horse from a neighbor – if his pride had let him. Heck, perhaps he'd raised a posse – although even after a year of living in the old-time, horse-powered world of the community, the idea struck Christine as so incongruous that it was hard to take seriously. But no matter how he was coming after her, she knew that if he regained his horses, it would only help him, and she had no desire to make his pursuit any easier. And anyway, regardless of the horses' usefulness either to herself or to the man or men who pursued her, she enjoyed their company and would be sorry to lose them.

Christine rode more slowly now, asking the mare to go no faster than a comfortable walking pace as they plodded onward through the never-ending upland forest. The riderless animals still followed placidly behind, and the going was still easy, with old-growth conifers that were widely spaced and very little underbrush, and although the twilight grew steadily deeper, a nearly full moon had already risen into a clear sky. Just as Christine began to wonder if it might after all make better sense to keep on riding through the night, they came upon the widest creek they'd had to cross so far. Like all the other smaller streams, it ran through the forest from west to east, and the horses would easily be able to wade across, but as Christine paused to consider the safest place to make the attempt, she became aware of a strange crashing sound that was coming from upstream. There was also something curious about the way the shadows fell across the land to the west, and as she peered through the trees in the fading light, it almost looked as if the forest had been enclosed by a high wall that marked its boundary.

She nudged the mare forward, and as she followed the creek upstream, the trees rapidly grew thinner. Before long she saw that the mysterious wall was in fact a small cliff, maybe twenty feet high, that ran along the far side of a strip of broken ground. Countless years ago, as the range of mountains thrust up ever higher, the land beneath the forest floor had slumped and the earth's crust had fractured in a landslip. Since then, eons of erosion had scoured the shattered rock and worn down the higher ground to form a channel, along which the creek now came babbling toward her along the edge of a blind, steep-sided, grassy valley about twenty yards wide and fifty yards long, tumbling over a short series of small but boisterous waterfalls and ending in a six-foot drop that sent the water crashing into a deep pool.

It was an idyllic place to make camp – and a practical one too. After the loose horses had splashed across the icy stream, Christine drove them into the valley without any difficulty. She hoped that the water and good grazing would be enough to keep them from straying, and by bedding down across the valley's entrance, she figured she had a good chance of waking up in time to head them off if they tried to get past her during the night.

As for the mare, Christine dared not let her wander free, and after making sure she was well-watered, she hitched the animal securely to the twisted trunk of a blasted pine within easy reach of a patch of lush summer grass.

With a horse blanket beneath her and a saddle for a pillow, Christine lay down on the ground. She'd eaten nothing since last night's fateful stew, and she knew that hunger would soon become a problem, but for now it couldn't be helped. Meanwhile at least she'd drunk her fill and the ground was no harder than the wooden floor she lay on every night. She fell asleep before the light of the sun had completely faded from the western sky and dreamed that she was riding horseback through a never-ending forest.

She was woken by a cold rain that fell from overcast skies just before dawn. The first thing she noticed was how hungry she was, and the next thing was that the loose horses were gone. She thought for a moment that her own horse had gone too, but when she leaped to her feet in a panic, she found the mare was still safely hitched, albeit chafing slightly to have been left outside in the sudden downpour.

There was nothing to be done about the missing horses. If she waited until daylight she might have been able to track them, but it was a doubtful enterprise at best, and she could hardly afford the delay. She reminded herself that she'd never meant to take them in the first place, but it was little consolation. Now that they were gone, their absence was still dispiriting. The dreary weather and the gnawing hunger in her belly didn't help either.

Christine peered once more into the shadows and failed once more to conjure any horses from the pools of darkness. The sun had not yet risen, but it was pointless to stay in the valley any longer, especially since it offered no shelter from the rain, so she saddled up the mare and broke camp.

Before she rode back into the forest and gave up completely on the other horses, she paused to listen one last time. But all she could hear was the waterfall, the leather and metal of the mare's bridle, and the hiss of rain falling on the patient earth. She might have listened all day, but she sensed the mare's impatience and nudged the horse forward.

The sun rose at last, invisible behind the clouds. Far below her, miles away on the steaming coastal plains, the day no doubt was hot and bright and humid, but at this elevation the light that trickled through the trees was pale and gave no warmth. The forest itself was subdued and listless and seemed almost devoid of life. She'd glimpsed birds and the occasional squirrel and other small game, but it would have been poor hunting even if she'd had a rifle or the material – and time – to fashion a snare.

Meanwhile the nagging pain of hunger dragged her spirits down and made her cranky and confused. She tried to remember how long it had been since she'd left the cabin. It felt like she'd been riding through these trees for several days, and she couldn't understand why she was only able to recall a single night. And where were the other horses? She could have sworn she'd started out with a whole string of them. Had they somehow gotten ahead of her?

And then a terrifying thought struck her: what if she'd ridden so far north that she'd already passed the desert? If she'd already come too far, then every step was now taking her further away. Perhaps she ought to turn around?

The mare sensed her indecision and walked to a standstill. Christine was so overwhelmed and lost that she longed to dismount and prop herself right there beside that very tree and sit and wait until her body failed from hunger and thirst and Valentine found her and buried her remains or simply left her there – it hardly mattered. But something deep inside her rebelled against surrender and she fought against this deadly impulse by urging the mare into a lope until the sheer exhilarating physical thrill of plunging downhill headlong through the forest blew every other thought away.

As her head cleared, she grew less afraid of missing her way. She knew the desert must after all still be far to the north and east, and also that it lay far below her present elevation, so with no set road to follow, she might as well begin the descent now instead of later.

The forest changed as she descended. There were fewer pines. Full-leafed trees grew thicker here and the light beneath them was a deeper green. These mossy woods stirred fevered memories of when the menfolk of the community had borne her semi-conscious from the fringes of the desert. The impression was so powerful that she became certain that she was in the right place and heading in the right direction. And then she chanced upon a trail.

In fact it formed such a natural path through the forest that she realized with a small shock that she'd already been following it for some minutes without even noticing. Unlike the countless meandering tracks that ran every which way to serve the smaller creatures of the woods, this one was too wide to have been made even by deer or bear, and although it was very poorly maintained, it had endured for however many scores of years because it had a sense of purpose.

The trail still led downhill, but much more slowly than her recent precipitous descent, and the topography reconfirmed the doubtful conviction of her memories: as before, she was trending northward, but now there was also a slight bias to the east. She reined in the mare to a walking pace to see if she could identify any of the muddled animal tracks that covered the ground, but while she'd hoped to find evidence of horses, the only hoof marks she found were made by deer. And then, at a place where the underbrush pressed in upon the trail, she saw a track beneath the bushes that was still untrampled and which could only have been made by a wheel.

There was no longer any question that this was the trail that led to the desert. Which meant that it was also the trail that Valentine would take if he meant to catch her – or head her off. She turned in the saddle, and although she could barely make out the mare's fresh hoof prints behind her, she knew that Valentine would read and understand them without any trouble. Still, he may yet be horseless and she'd been making good time. Her best hope as always was to keep pushing forward, and she made up her mind that from now on, she'd keep riding with only short breaks for the mare. She would camp for the night again only when she'd reached the safety of the desert. Until then, she could sleep in the saddle.

She was just about to dig her heels into the mare's side

and push the animal into a trot when she saw what she thought must be an hallucination:

Amid the oaks and birch and lindens and sycamores, there stood a solitary, mighty, ancient chestnut tree. The trail passed directly beneath its enormous boughs and there were signs of long-abandoned campsites nearby.

She drew closer and saw where bears had scratched their claw marks in the bark, and she noticed that here, more than any other place in the forest, the air overhead was filled with birdsong and the chattering of squirrels. It was impossible to guess how the tree had come to be there, but over the years it had grown to become a waypoint for every living creature that lived in these woods or journeyed through them.

The ground was covered with empty brown husks from previous generations of chestnuts, and the tree itself was full of tantalizing clusters that in another month or so would ripen into this year's crop. But Christine was ravenous, and the sticky milk-white liquid inside the unformed chestnuts still counted as food. The lowest clusters dangled more than eight feet from the ground, but she reached them easily just by riding underneath. The green nuts were a lot easier to open too. She picked them at her leisure and ate them on horseback. She'd meant to pace herself, but it was a solid five minutes before she finally paused from squeezing the nuts until they burst and then sucking out the sweet fluid from within.

It was messy but satisfying.

Her stomach gurgled and swung into action and a small twinge of pain reminded her once again to slow down. She remembered hearing something about almonds containing cyanide, and wondered briefly if unripe chestnuts might also be toxic. Perhaps that was the reason why people only ate them roasted in the wintertime?

Another twinge from her abdomen and, poisoned or not, she realized she needed to dismount. On foot she felt suddenly vulnerable. There might have been no-one within fifty miles, but after she'd hitched the mare, she looked suspiciously in all directions before she withdrew behind the cover of a bush.

She emerged two minutes later feeling shaken and exhausted, but also somehow stronger. She was going to make it. For the first time since Valentine had clapped the manacle on her wrist, she felt in control.

But the mare was not where she had left it.

A lurching dread swept over her. She rushed forward, her eyes desperately sweeping the space beneath the tree for any sign of the missing animal – and there she was, grazing placidly on another bush. With Valentine beside her.

Christine ran.

She had no idea which way she was going, or whether it was uphill or down, or how fast she was running or for how long she ran, but inevitably, after an appropriate interval of time, she felt the heavy body of a human male fall on top of her and as she struggled to get free, her wrists were efficiently bound together and then she was pulled to her feet. She resisted and struggled and fought against every tug on the rope that he was using to control her and then something struck her head and everything went black and when she came awake again she was tied to a tree.

It was still daylight and the rain had stopped and it might have been some time in the late afternoon. Her hands were tied behind her back and her left hand felt strangely light as though some part of it were missing and then she realized that the manacle had been removed. Her head hurt but she was surprised to find that it was a vague, unfocused, dull ache that she could almost ignore. Mainly her skull just felt raw and very fragile.

Her mind seemed to be clear. She understood that Valentine had found her and caught her and she was once again his prisoner. She saw that he'd made camp and that he had six horses – the mare, another horse she'd never seen before and the four loose horses, all of which had now been fitted with rope bridles – and that he'd started a small cook-fire in the lee of the chestnut's giant trunk.

It bothered her to think that the fire would harm the tree, and she wished that she could douse the flames. There were many other things she could have worried about, but at least her sympathy for the tree helped to distract her from her own fate – and especially from wondering why Valentine would choose to camp here for the night instead of taking her back to the cabin immediately, hogtied on one of the horses.

She watched him eat a large supper. Perhaps it was just because she was so hungry herself, but it felt like he was eating an unusually extravagant amount just to torture her. In any case he seemed to have brought an abundance of supplies. She was almost flattered: he'd evidently anticipated that it might take many days to run her down.

He paused once in his eating and, carrying his plate, he came to her. For a fleeting moment, Christine was consumed by the idea that he was bringing her food, but no: it was only to check her bonds. Her betrayed stomach groaned with disappointment. She thought of asking him for water, and maybe she would have if she'd thought he would have obliged. Or then again, maybe she wouldn't. If she was as fucked as she thought she was, then she could at least go out with her head high. To hell with Valentine.

So when he came to her a short time later and proffered his canteen, she merely looked away and didn't even condescend to shake her head.

Without a word, Valentine left her and went to fetch the borrowed horse that he was riding. He led it back to the chestnut tree, where he unhitched a coil of rope from the saddle. He tied one end to the saddle tree and threw the other end over a sturdy horizontal bough. Christine watched him with growing horror.

"My God, Valentine. Please, no. You can't."

She hoped she hadn't said the words aloud. Her continued silence would at least be one small victory. It might even unsettle him to finally have to deal with someone as taciturn as himself.

"I reckon I told you the way we deal with horse thieves. But it don't make no difference if you remember or not. I mean to hang you just the same."

It didn't take him long to tie the hangman's knot. He led the horse forward and the noose rose into the air until it hung eight feet from the ground – the same height as the lowest chestnuts. Satisfied, he backed the horse up again – a maneuver with which the horse was evidently unfamiliar, and which proceeded one or two steps at a time as the horse struggled to understand what was required of it.

At last the noose lay slack upon the ground. Valentine picked it up with both hands as if it were some kind of mystical offering. He gauged the distance to where Christine sat trussed and helpless: the rope was far too short to reach, so he put the noose down again. He took out his knife and came over to her.

Christine refused to look up as he approached, but her attention followed his every move as he went behind her and cinched a loop of rawhide around her wrists. He cut her loose from the tree that she was tied to, and with the knife still in his hand, he grabbed the back of the ridiculous dress that she was still wearing and hauled her to her feet. He pushed her into motion, and the way he ushered her toward the waiting rope seemed almost gentle, although perhaps he was only being cautious.

They reached the noose.

Christine felt Valentine hesitate as he mentally rehearsed the slightly complicated maneuver that would be needed if he were to place the noose around her neck without letting her hands go free. The borrowed horse snorted with impatience and turned its head to look at them with rolling eyes as if anxious for the hanging to proceed. Valentine held the cinch of rawhide tight with one hand as he stooped and picked up the noose with the hand that held the knife. He straightened up again with the rope now safely in his hand, and in that moment Christine felt – or imagined that she felt – a barely perceptible relaxation run through his body.

She waited. Valentine draped the noose upon her shoulder. Awkwardly, still clutching his knife, he took hold of the loop of rope, and as he raised it over her to drop around her neck, she cried out with all the force of her lungs and plunged away from him regardless of the immediate wrenching pain in her wrists and shoulders and the horse responded to her yell by also starting forward and jerking the noose upward. Valentine clung to it reflexively and dropped his knife and let go his hold upon her wrists as the noose slipped tight around his fingers and he was pulled abruptly three feet into the air.

Rendered powerless, as if a blundering hangman had sent him prematurely through the scaffold floor, he dangled like a piñata and writhed and jerked and raged. Christine felt the enormity of his frustration when one of his blind kicks slammed into her shoulder as she lunged toward the fallen knife. Face down in the chestnut husks and leaf-mold, she worked in desperate haste to free her wrists from the rawhide until at last, with unspeakable gratitude and relief, her arms were free and she rolled across the ground and picked up the knife.

"Die, you bastard."

She stabbed him multiple times. Attacking from the side, she struck him in his calves at first. As he lost blood and grew weaker, she worked further up his legs to his ass and his genitals until his screams turned to sobs and his defensive kicks and contortions became no more than twitches. At last she plunged the knife into his stomach, just below his ribs, as high as she could reach. She wrapped both hands around the knife's handle, and hung onto it with all her weight. She felt a spasm of resistance, then something gave. Knotted sheets of muscle tore apart as the knife cut all the way down until its point struck bone and the blade deflected. The knife slipped out of Valentine's body, and without its support, Christine fell to the ground. Above her, she saw a strange lopsided bulge under Valentine's blood-soaked shirt and knew that it contained his entrails. She squirmed away and giggled as her overloaded mind looped round and round a single thought: how lucky she was that Valentine had always been a man who wore his shirts tucked in.

The whicker of a horse brought Christine back to her senses. The bloodied knife was still in her hand. She tossed it aside, then thought better of it and picked it up again and wiped it clumsily on the leaf litter. Her face was wet with tears and streaks of blood from where she'd rubbed her eyes. Swiftly glancing several times in Valentine's direction to reassure herself that he was still there and still safely dead, she went to the horse and backed it up until the weight of his body was set upon the ground and the rope was slack enough for her to unhitch it from the pommel.

She freed Valentine's pale, blue, dislocated fingers from the other end of the rope, untied the noose and tied the coiled rope to the horse's saddle. She found the half-empty canteen and mounted up.

The evening light was fading now, and she had no clear idea of where she was headed, but the compulsion to keep moving – and in particular to keep moving away from Valentine's slumped corpse – was overwhelming. The horse seemed content to make its own way obliquely downhill, and that was fine with Christine. She dozed in the saddle. The horse ambled on.

At times during the night, Christine drifted into wakefulness. Her mind felt clear. She wondered if the desert would be as bad as she remembered it.

CHAPTER 13

The desert was exactly as bad as she remembered it.

At the edge of the forest she forced the reluctant horse to leave the security of the trees and climb the first gentle slope of scrubland toward the open desert. Even before she could see it, she felt it as a palpable thing. At the top of the rise she sat her horse and gazed out at the emptiness that lay ahead. With the sun just risen an hour ago, the desert was already full of deadly light and air, and instead of the madness of walking out into this vast and shimmering furnace, she wondered if perhaps it might be better after all simply to turn back. After all, now that Valentine was dead... And perhaps Nathaniel...

Or perhaps the unwilling horse was somehow controlling her thoughts. She laughed a rueful, scornful, only slightly hysterical laugh.

"Sorry, horse."

She patted its neck and tried to visualize the desert crossing. Although the details were hazy, it seemed possible. She felt bad about the horse, but she rationalized that one or even both of them might very well survive. In what felt like full consciousness of what she was doing, she accepted the path she knew she had to take, urged the horse forward and stepped irrevocably into the desert.

Christine understood how travelers came to walk in circles and she knew how to prevent it, but when she tried to apply the trick of fixing her gaze upon a distant object and walking straight toward it, she found it was impossible: there were no distant objects, only a fierce and immediate sensory barrage that crowded in upon her with an austere palette of graded colors and degrees of luminosity, from the rippling black puddle of darkness that slipped along on the ground beneath her horse to the sterilizing whiteness of the sun above. Meanwhile the light and heat in any case conspired with the terrain to dissolve even the crispest horizon into ambiguity. She also was dismayed to find that, despite the lateness of the season, within three hours of sunrise the angle of the light that fell upon their heads became so close to vertical that their shadows were too short to clearly indicate direction.

So she stopped the horse and climbed down from the saddle into the superheated layer of air that clung to the desert floor. She took a swallow from the canteen and poured dribbles of water into the palm of her hand and gave them to the horse to assuage and reassure it, only to find that she resented every drop that fell from the animal's lips and splashed into tiny wasteful craters on the burning sand.

With the canteen once again safely stoppered, she built a framework out of the sticks that she had carried with her from the forest for this very purpose. She contrived to raise the frame a few feet from the ground and laid out her blood- and mud-caked dress upon it. It was absurdly, stiflingly hot in the shade beneath this makeshift screen, but she crawled beneath it anyway to shield herself from the murderous rays of the sun. Struggling to breath, she drifted into semi-consciousness and passed the rest of the day in something more like a fever than sleep.

Exhausted by many hours of arduous slumber, she slept on well into the evening, until long after the sun had left the sky, savoring at last even while asleep the delicious coolness of the night air. Eventually she awoke, almost with a shiver, and she was glad enough to get dressed once again. She was also glad to see that the dress's hideous stains were barely visible in the moonlight, and she managed to put it on with hardly a shudder. She dismantled the frame of sticks, took her bearings from the moon and the stars, and in inexplicably good spirits, she mounted up and set off once again across the floor of the desert.

Apart from a steadily growing conviction that she was making absolutely no progress at all, the night proceeded uneventfully. She thought she remembered that Valentine had been careful to avoid crossing the desert by night, but she had no memory of why that might be. The discrepancy worried her, but when the sun rose and her horse continued to walk steadily forward in exactly the same way as before, she was finally able to put it out of her mind.

As the grueling day wore on, the flatness of the desert subdued her. She ached to be back in the forest, where every tree had its own movement and life, its own identity and context. Here there was nothing but bleakness extending outward in every direction. There was no distinction between objects. She felt the grinding malevolent weight of the place as more than a mere abstraction, and when she recalled her sickness on the outbound journey, she began to wonder if the desert itself had some mysterious power to make her ill. Everything it touched was left seared and blistered: her senses, her personality, her will. It was hard to hold on to her thoughts. She found she could no longer remember whether she'd resolved to travel by night or day, or if or why it was so important one way or the other. She tried to remember when and why and how she had entered into this hellscape. How could such a thing ever have come about?

Basted in sunlight, her brain bubbled and simmered through the rest of the day in similar fashion and only cooled again when the sun wrapped itself in the horizon and at last slipped out of the world. In the merciful darkness, she recovered herself enough to make camp. She sucked the last trace of dampness from the canteen — there was nothing left for her to share with the horse — and spent the night huddled fully clothed in a small hollow that she'd scooped out with her own hands in the lee of a low ridge.

The following day brought no respite. The unwatered horse was stoical as only a beast can be. It blinked and squinted and bore her closer and closer to the desert's further side even as it shriveled almost visibly in the blazing sunlight. She was the cause of all the animal's suffering, but she had no remedy. In the evening, when she made camp as before, she could not bring herself to hobble it. If it had thought to wander, she would have willingly let it go to ease her conscience, but the faithful beast stayed near to her and she fell asleep to the sound of its breathing.

She woke to find the horse had died.

She registered the fact and then tried very hard not to think about it. Dawn had already broken, so she left the horse and walked toward the sun. She plodded after it so doggedly that even when it climbed too high for her to aim at, she kept going anyway, careless now of whether she was moving in circles or not.

She saw a shape in the distance and eventually realized that her feet were carrying her toward it even in the absence of any conscious decision on her part. The object — whatever it was — lay somewhat to the north of her intended path, but after so many hours of moving through a meaningless, undifferentiated wasteland with nothing more than an imaginary compass to guide her, the siren call of a concrete thing was irresistible; it would have drawn her to itself whatever its bearing, even if she thought it was leading her astray.

As she drew closer, the details and the scale of the thing remained ambiguous, and waves of vertigo swept over her. The whole experience felt unreal. Even its greenish-gray color seemed unlikely. Until at last – and not without a certain disappointment that her death had been postponed – she saw that it was neither a mirage nor an hallucination nor yet some squatting demon conjured there to carry her away, but simply, unmistakably, a sprawling clump of prickly pear.

She swept aside a dim memory that told her not to eat or drink too quickly and plunged ahead. Luckily, even though Valentine's knife made relatively fast and easy work of harvesting the red fruit and cutting away the spine-tufted skin, she found that no matter how frantically she wanted to eat, it took an infinity of painstaking chewing to separate the pulp from the myriad seeds. After half an hour of frustratingly slow gorging, her stomach began to protest and she came up for air. She was in no hurry after all: the patient opuntia wasn't going anywhere; it would wait for her. She felt luxurious and generous. She wanted to share her bounty with the horse and looked around to see where it was, only to remember that it had died – died because of her and then she had left it – and she was overcome with sorrow.

More than anything, she needed to believe in her own innocence. The violence she'd perpetrated on her violent husband was easily excused, but when it came to the horse... Shuddering with guilt, she sobbed like a child banished to her room and left alone, hopeless and bewildered, to cry herself to sleep in the face of an endless, unjust timeout.

She woke up sticky eyed from a blank dream and found herself immersed once more in the desert's bone-dry reality. On the trunk of a fallen branch of the cactus, inches from her face, she saw the scars of knife marks – some ancient and none more recent than a year ago – and she dimly misremembered how the two of them – her and Valentine, man and wife – had come to this place when she was sick and he had carved slices from the soapy leaves and fruit for her to eat.

The silvery-gray scars reminded her of the marks she'd made with her brown and green crayons on the wallpaper of her childhood bedroom. Could it somehow have been this very cactus that she'd been trying to draw? She felt a mystical wave of completeness, of closure, sweep over her, and she rose to her feet as if reborn with a new sense of identity and purpose .

She turned away from the cactus and she walked. If her body took any notice of the sun or the moon or the stars or whatever celestial bodies happened to be in the sky at that moment, or if it performed any calculations of direction or probable distance, she was unaware of it. She simply walked. On and on, unerringly. Her mind – her conscious self – checked out completely, refusing even to rise to the level of a passive observer, preferring instead to play the part of a confidently dozing passenger until at last she came fully awake in the dawn of a whole new day and found herself trudging through a landscape of low dunes where patches of sere grass struggled to hold the loose sand together against the gentle ravages of the morning breeze.

She had reached the fringes of the desert.

Each dune she passed was bigger and looked more permanent than the last. She found a track and took it. It meandered lazily between the hills, and drove her almost to despair with all the extra distance she had to walk, but overall she judged that it was definitely taking her east. And then, around the middle of the morning, she looked up from the dusty river of churned-up earth that she was doggedly following and suddenly, spread out a few hundred feet below her in a serene vista, she saw nothing but farmland stretching all the way to the sea.

She'd made it.

The emotional rush alone was nearly enough to kill her. She wanted to laugh and cry and run... but most of all she didn't want to die, and she didn't want her dead body to be found by the side of the trail three weeks from now with a rapturous grin on its face. So she choked back her feelings, and allowing herself only a grim smile of satisfaction, she kept on walking.

After taking almost an hour to descend to the plain and then another two hours to walk across open fields that increasingly showed signs of being under the plow, she reached a plot of land where rows of parched corn stood under the full sun next to the deep green shade of a grove of plantains. Beyond the plantains a thin trickle of smoke rose steadily and almost vertically into the hazy air. Christine had spotted this smoke when she'd first gazed out over the plain from the edge of the hills, and together with the nearby rich, dark patch of green, she took it as an unmistakable sign of human habitation. Farther off she'd been able to make out actual buildings – ranches, homesteads and even apartment blocks – but this thread of smoke was closer and she'd marked it as her destination.

On the far side of the plantains, there was a kitchen garden and beyond that, a modest adobe hut. The whole place appeared deserted, but the same unbroken thread of smoke came up through the roof of the building and kept climbing up into the sky, so Christine picked her way across the garden and went toward it. The hut was partly sunk into the earth, and it stood beneath three palm trees that were neither date nor coconut – they bore no fruit at all. Christine was strangely moved to think that the people who subsisted here had taken the trouble to plant trees whose only function seemed to be ornamental.

Around the corner of the hut, she came upon a woman weaving a basket and two small children playing in the dirt. They were all sitting in the shade of a palm-leaf thatch, and now that Christine understood the true purpose of the palm trees, she felt a jar of something that resembled disappointment. But still, the tranquil scene was so compelling that she stumbled forward immediately and didn't even think to call out any greeting as she approached. When the woman finally noticed her, she screamed in real alarm at Christine's sudden silent arrival in their midst.

The children ran to hide behind their mother, while the startled woman crossed herself and murmured something about Dios. Christine felt bad about the scare she'd accidentally given them, but she was surprised that they continued to be so fearful. Surely the shock should have worn off by now? Then she saw the way that they were staring at her, and she realized that with her outlandish clothes, torn and blood-caked as they were, even the way she looked must be alarming. She reached out her hand.

"Por favor..."

She stopped because she had no more Spanish and also because in any case she had no clear idea of what she wanted to say.

The woman likewise didn't know what was required of her. She shook her head and without taking her eyes off Christine, she called out:

"Ramon!"

The barefoot Indios man whose name was Ramon came out of the hut with their third and eldest child, a boy of maybe fourteen years. For a moment Ramon just stood there, blinking in the sun. He stared at Christine then went inside again and came back out with a metal cup full of water. She couldn't remember if she was thirsty or not, but she took a sip and thanked him and then started to cry.

Their apprehension vanished instantly, and Christine was swept up in an effusion of hospitality. They made her sit down in the shade and fetched more water. The woman, who was mortified to think that she had mistaken their guest for a demon, brought out a pastry on a china plate and offered Christine cigarettes. She made her youngest child put on some clothes and then had all three children present Christine with a basket of some kind of local fruit – a fruit which Christine had never seen before, and which she found impossibly delicious.

Now that the woman was no longer terrified, she'd been regarding Christine with curiosity and concern, and now she pointed at Christine's belly and mimed an advanced state of pregnancy and then pointed at her own children for good measure. Her performance was a question, and Christine answered accordingly:

"Si."

The woman knew by then that Christine's Spanish was rudimentary and she asked no more questions, but she tut-tutted to herself and launched into an involved conversation with her husband. When they spoke together, they used a language that was older than Spanish and even more impenetrable, but Christine didn't need to understand the words to know that they were talking about her, and she guessed that they were trying to figure out what to do with her.

She felt safe and full and sleepy, and she trusted these people completely. It was so tempting to put herself entirely in their hands...

But they had done so much already, it seemed unfair to burden them any further. She was also very much aware – as they were not – that her return to civilization might not be straightforward, and she was afraid of bringing all kinds of un-deserved and unknown consequences down upon their heads. So when she heard Ramon clearly enunciate for a second time the word "Federales", she let their conversation continue on for two or three more sentences and when she was sure they'd left the cops behind, she interrupted with a word of her own:

"Taxi."

They protested extravagantly – and Christine was relieved because she wasn't sure if they would even know the word. It was also clear that both Ramon and his wife in fact thought that calling a cab was a good idea. The next problem was how to do it. They had no land line or cell phone and the nearest payphone was out on the highway, which as Christine understood it, was itself "many kilometers", or a good taxi ride away.

The eldest son made a suggestion, and when it was met with enthusiastic approval, he set out immediately across the fields, trotting toward a small group of huts about two miles away. Ramon and his wife congratulated each other on having such a son, and bursting with pride, they encouraged Christine to share in their appreciation of the boy's genius.

A short while later, they heard the sound of an engine, and their son and another slightly older boy came riding back up to the hut on the back of a dirt bike. The other boy was introduced to Christine as a neighbor's son who sometimes did some work in town, and he had come because he owned a cell phone. The phone was passed around and marveled at and generally admired, and any shortcomings that it might have had were readily excused. The call was placed, and after an extended negotiation and much use of the word "gringa", it was Ramon's wife who finally persuaded the cab company to send out one of their cars to an intersection not far from their present location.

When everything had been arranged, it occurred to Christine that she had no money. She said nothing – she was certain that if Ramon knew, he would insist on paying, and there was no way that she was going to let any of these people pick up the tab for a taxi ride all the way back to Tulum – and simply accepted that if the worst came to the worst, she might end up having to deal with the Federales after all.

Christine hadn't understood the arrangements that had been made with the cab company, and she wrongly assumed that the cab would simply be driving out to the hut. So she was confused when the cell phone rang about an hour later, and after everyone had expressed a favorable opinion of the ring tone, the neighbor's son took the call and relayed the information that the cab had arrived.

The two boys took off on the dirt bike again and came back fifteen minutes later followed by a yellow taxi-cab. The bike stopped in the middle of the dirt track that ran past the front of Ramon's hut, and the cab pulled up behind it. The cab driver stepped out of his vehicle. He was an unshaven man in a spectacularly colorful shirt, and he engaged in a prolonged and lively argument with the two boys and then with Ramon and then with Ramon's wife, at first successively and then all at once.

Just as things began to quiet down, the oldest son pointed toward Tulum, and seemed to be confused as to why the cab was pointing in the opposite direction. Everyone immediately agreed that the gringa could hardly be expected to begin her journey by setting off in the wrong direction.

The driver got behind the wheel and turned the car around so that it was facing the right way. He then made a big deal out of starting the meter, both to demonstrate his scrupulous honesty and also to make it clear that no more concessions would be made. He and the gringa had now entered into a binding contract, at the end of which, after he'd fulfilled his contractual obligations in a satisfactory manner, he would get paid.

The family ushered Christine into the back seat of the cab, and under instructions from his mother, the middle child presented her with another small basket of fruit. The cab jolted away and the rear door swung closed and the fruit fell to the floor and rolled in every direction.

"Senor! Senor!"

Christine lurched forward and grabbed the collar of the

driver's colorful shirt.

"Por favor! Stop! Please stop!"

Her mind flew back to a similar desperate plea that she once made to Valentine. But this time, even though the driver did not completely understand her, he brought the car to a halt and waited sullenly while she got out of the car and climbed back into the front seat. As she sat, she mimed for him the exaggerated contour of her pregnancy, and he was suddenly full of a thousand apologies. Dios and Madonna were both invoked and he kissed the Saint Christopher that was hanging from the rear view and encouraged her to do the same. Before he set off again, he got out of the car and ran around to close the passenger door for her, after which he eased the vehicle forward at a snail's pace and apologized profusely for every bump and pothole.

Eventually they reached paved highway, and on the rest of the way back to Tulum they drove at normal speed. The driver surreptitiously turned to look at her every now and then, and seemed embarrassed whenever Christine caught him doing so. He must have been curious about her appearance and her circumstances, but even if he could have gotten around the language barrier, as a professional driver, he seemed to follow some special code and probably didn't think it was his place to ask. She didn't know what she would have told him anyway.

As they came into the outskirts of the city, he seemed to grow uncomfortable and his driving became more hesitant. At each intersection he kept repeating a word in Spanish – a common word that Christine recognized, but she couldn't remember what it meant. He tried some other words:

"Medicales? Hopitale?"

At last Christine understood. She shook her head and said "no" firmly – she only wanted to be clear, and she was sorry when he shrank back like a scolded dog – and she gave him the address of the villa that she'd shared with Emma. As he checked and digested this information, he looked at her strangely and even a little fearfully, but now that his immediate question had been answered, he once again drove with a sense of purpose.

Christine gazed out of the window and tried to remember how the streets fit together. They drove past places and landmarks that she recognized, and as always, there seemed to be people everywhere. Everything looked normal. In so many ways, the city looked just like it had when she'd left it. But now, after barely a year away, the everyday world on the other side of the taxicab's windshield was so massively unlike everything she'd grown used to that it was like watching life on an alien planet.

They reached the sea, and turned to follow the road that ran just behind the shacks and expensive properties and groves of coconut palm and casuarina that fringed the beach. They almost missed the villa. Its wrought iron gates were closed and the high pink walls on either side were overgrown with vines. A screen of weeds had sprung up between the road and the driveway. The place had clearly been abandoned, but this was the address that his fare had given him, so the taxi-driver dutifully stopped and walked over to the gates and rattled them to see if they would open.

Christine stayed in the cab. She could see the ruined gardens through the gates. She remembered that when she'd lived here, the landscaped grounds had been assiduously manicured by two smiling brothers who derived an almost spiritual satisfaction from their work. She wondered if they ever came back and whether it would make them sad or merely philosophical to see their garden in its present state. She hoped at least they'd been well paid. And she hoped that she would think of something to say to the taxi driver before he came back to the car and demanded the money that she now owed him.

But now she saw that the driver had been engaged in

conversation by an old man who'd wandered out from his shack across the street to see why a taxi had pulled up outside the derelict villa. Christine got out of the car and joined them.

"Senora Christine!"

The old man remembered her and somehow even knew her name. He gestured at her and turned to the taxi driver and launched into a long explanation in Spanish of who she was and how they knew each other. After that he evidently asked the driver about her clothes and general appearance because they both kept pointing at her and the driver kept shaking his head and saying "no lo sé". The driver's only contribution was to demonstrate to the old man that Christine was pregnant. After this exchange, the driver apologized and took hold of Christine's arm and led her gently back to the cab where he pointed at the meter.

Christine told him she didn't have any money.

The driver clearly understood her, but he was reluctant to believe that it could possibly be true. He obliged her to state and restate the situation again and again, and still he protested that he was at a loss to understand her.

The old man came over to see what they were arguing about and the driver stated the exact number of pesos that were showing on the meter and invited the old man to pay him instead. The old man refused and the driver expressed his exasperation. Then he turned to Christine.

"He says, how can you not have any money?"

"You speak English!?"

"A little, yes."

"Senor, please tell him that my friend was going to pay, but she doesn't live here any more. And tell him that I'm sorry and I'll pay him when I can."

"Yes, nobody lives here any more."

"Do you know where they've gone? My friend, Emma, do you know where she is?"

"Emma, yes, I remember her name."

"Where can I find her?"

The old man shook his head and waved his hand to deflect the question.

"No lo sé, no lo sé."

"What about Luiz? You must know Luiz, right?"

The old man looked at her sadly, and again he shook his head. And then:

"Do you carry his child?"

"What? No."

"It is well."

"What? What do you mean? Why is it well? And what about Benito? 'Nito? You remember him?"

"Ah, Benito, si."

Christine stared at him. Then why the fuck hadn't he said so in the first place?

"You want to see Benito?"

"You know where he lives?"

"He's not hard to find."

"Well, so that's good then, right?"

She hadn't meant it as a rhetorical question, but instead of answering, the old man turned to the driver and switched into Spanish. The driver had been growing increasingly hopeful and was very curious to hear what the old man had to tell him. But once he understood which Benito they'd been talking about, his anxiety peaked all over again.

The old man translated one of his concerns:

"He says, are you sure that Benito will give you his money?"

She had been sure – right up until the old man asked her. But what else was she going to do?

"Sure."

Christine had never been to Benito's place — she'd only even been to Luiz's place once, and that was in the very early days — but she knew his style, so it didn't surprise her when the cab pulled up outside a tasteful and expensive property in a very expensive part of town.

All the security didn't surprise her either.

"They won't let you in, so just wait out here."

"Si, si."

The cab driver understood well enough what she was saying, and by now he was resigned to the possibility that he might never get paid. He had no intention of even trying to go inside. He only prayed that no-one would come out and shoot him just for sitting there, although he accepted that that too was in the hands of God.

The cab's arrival had already been noted, and when Christine walked up to the building's glass-fronted, box-like security lobby and buzzed to be let in, there was already an extra security guy waiting inside. He'd been summoned up from somewhere deep in the building especially to deal with her, and he was wearing an extremely nice suit. When he saw from up close how Christine was dressed, he hesitated for a good ten seconds before he told the regular security guy behind the desk to buzz her in.

"Thanks. Look, I know I look like shit and I'm sorry about the clothes but I'm an old friend of Benito's and guess what? This is kind of an emergency."

The guy in the nice suit waved the desk guy forward to pat her down.

"Benito isn't in."

"Can I wait?"

"Not in here. Maybe you should have called ahead."

"Do I look like I have a phone?"

The suit-guy took a cell phone from the desk and gave it to her.

"I don't know his number."

"You're a friend of Benito and you don't know his personal number."

The man shrugged, as if to say: you see how this looks. He gestured at her swollen belly.

"Is that his?"

"No."

"OK."

"How about Emma? Is she here?"

"You know Emma?"

"Yes! Yes I do! And no, I don't remember her number but I know it ended in eight-three-three. Can you call her?"

The man nodded to the guy behind the desk, who called a number on his cell phone, checked that it was ringing and then gave her the phone.

She held it to her ear. A woman picked up.

"Hello?"

"Emma. It's Christine."

CHAPTER 14

Emma had news of her own: shortly after Christine had left with Valentine, she'd persuaded Benito to marry her.

She said that Christine would die when she saw the ring – it was a real monster – and then she told her in a hushed, half-disbelieving voice that unless she had 'Nito's express permission, she wasn't allowed to take it out of the building. Christine wondered if she had ever done so. The Emma that she knew – the old, unmarried Emma from their beach villa days – certainly would have, but the woman sitting across from her seemed to have grown uncomfortable with the whole topic, and Christine didn't ask.

There had been other changes too. Luiz was dead – or he had disappeared, which amounted to the same thing – and Benito had stepped into his shoes so smoothly that it was almost like the whole thing had been planned.

"I know he'd never hurt me though. I trust him completely. I mean after all, hey, I married the guy, right? To be honest, it's been a little rough these past few months, but I guess that's what happens. They say every couple goes through the same thing."

Emma and Christine were catching up and drinking coffee at the kitchen table of a small, functional apartment that Benito said he rarely used. Christine originally thought she'd only be living there for a few days while she recovered, but she'd been physically well for several weeks now, and the new unspoken understanding was that Benito was letting her stay on until the baby was born. He was taking care of all her medical arrangements and expenses too. So even though Emma was happy to see her old friend, and glad too that she had survived an ordeal that she found almost incomprehensible, Christine's return – and Benito's generosity – had also reawakened all their old rivalry, and Emma now felt more threatened by her than ever.

Which is why she was pleased as well as disappointed when she found that Christine just wasn't that much fun any more. She'd bounced right back from all that backwoods shit she'd been through, and Emma kept waiting for her to start partying like she used to, but it never happened. Probably it was the baby messing with her hormones. Clubbing was out of the question too, because with the due date now only about a month away, the best Christine could manage was a deeply unsexy waddle.

On the other hand Emma also knew that Benito, like all Mexican men, thought that motherhood was only half a step down from sainthood.

"So does it feel weird?"

"You're seriously asking? Because look at me. OK, you can't really see me and I'm not going to stand up, but I know you remember what I look like – and how is that not going to feel weird? And you know what? I'll tell you how it feels: heavy is how it feels."

"I envy you in a way."

"I envy you too, in a way."

"What's that supposed to mean?"

"I don't know. Like at least you fit through doors. I thought you didn't want kids?"

"I'm not sure I do. But you look so great, and I think

'Nito would like it. And it might help too, you know? With our relationship? You know what it is yet?"

"I've been told it's a girl."

Christine wondered if Miriam's prediction would really turn out to be true, while Emma's imagination flew forward twenty years to a time when she'd be in her forties and Christine's daughter would eclipse her even more completely than Christine did right now.

Several days after Emma's visit, Benito came to the apartment. It was the first time that Christine had seen him since she'd been back. She led him through to the kitchen and offered him coffee, which he declined. She sat at the table and invited him to join her, but he remained standing. Or leaning. He would have paced if there'd been enough room.

'Nito, I don't even know where to begin. All this – the apartment, the doctors. You literally saved my life here – both our lives – taking care of me like this."

"De nada. It's really good to see you again, Christine. And you're looking great. Is everything good with you and the baby?"

"It's all on schedule and we're both doing great."

"That's good. Anything you need, you let me know. Just tell Emma."

"Sure. Thanks. I will."

"No need for any surprises this time, eh? Because when you left before, we heard this crazy story. That you ran off with some cowboy..."

"You know the story's true."

"Luiz was going to come after you."

"The guy's dead, Benito."

"Really?"

"I killed him myself, so yeah, really."

"I always liked you, Christine."

"Yeah, I know. I always liked you too. But Emma's my friend."

"I should have said something sooner. Then perhaps things might have turned out different."

"Perhaps. I guess we'll never know."

"Would you like to work for me?"

"Do I have to?"

"It was just a question."

"I can say no and you won't be insulted?"

"Sure. You can say no."

"Then no. But thanks for asking. And I appreciate that you're giving me a choice."

"Of course. And you can think about it. You'll be around for a few more weeks, right? Let me know if you change your mind."

A few weeks later, Christine called Emma from the hospital.

"Emma? Hey, it's Christine. I need to ask a favor."

"Okay."

"It's a big one."

Christine wasn't sure if asking Benito to buy her a car was really such a big favor or not, but even if it only came in at a fraction of what he'd already covered in medical bills, it still wasn't the sort of thing she felt she should take for granted.

Emma said she'd see what she could do, but she'd been careful not make any promises. In fact though she was more than happy to push the idea with Benito because a car would take Christine back to the US and out of their lives forever and then everyone would be happy. And Benito, although he'd be sorry to see Christine go, was also glad enough to tie up any loose ends, as well as regain unrestricted access to his apartment, which at that time had several kilos of cocaine hidden behind its walls. The car itself – the money and the paperwork – was part of what he did, and although he was amused to discover how much more expensive and difficult it was to buy and register a vehicle legally, everything went through without a problem.

Early in the morning of the day after Christine got out of the hospital, a man who worked for Benito came round to the apartment to drop off the car and the keys and also to hand her an unmarked, sealed envelope. She opened the envelope as soon as he'd left and found it contained five hundred US dollars.

She was already packed – a single overnight bag, only half full – and it was clear by now that no one was coming to see her off, so she agonized for a few minutes on what farewell message to leave, and eventually settled on "Thanks, C", which she wrote on the back of the empty envelope and left on the kitchen table together with the keys to the apartment.

Parked out on the street she found a silver, nearly-new, Japanese compact. The remote key locking feature didn't seem to work, but it started first time. She had a pretty good idea of which road to take out of town, and fifteen minutes later she was turning onto a major highway and passing a sign that notified travelers that they were heading toward "el Norte".

She figured it was two days to the Texas border and toyed with the idea of driving straight through the night or maybe just pulling over and sleeping in the car, but when it started to get dark, she checked into a decent-looking motel as she'd known all along that she would. The trip so far had been uneventful and she wanted to keep it that way.

Next day, she checked out early and made good time and reached Matamoros by mid-afternoon. The tailback at the border crossing was bad, but not as bad as it had been last time she'd come through that way, and it was still light when she got to the front of the line and was waved forward into an inspection bay.

The immigration officer tapped on the glass and Christine wound down her window and found herself looking at the same mirrored aviator wraparounds with the same Latina behind them.

The officer checked her papers.

"Ms Cooper?"

"That's right."

"You came through here once before?"

"Maybe a couple of years ago."

"Thought so. Never forget a face, though with some of them, I wish I could. Glad to see you worked things out with your husband."

"What?!"

"I mean your little girl there. It's a girl, right?"

"Yeah, it's a girl. Emily Ruth. And yeah, I guess we did."

"I hope I didn't speak out of line?"

"No, it's OK."

The Latina returned Christine's passport.

"You're all set. Welcome back, Ms Cooper. You have a great day now."

"Thanks."

The Latina slapped the car roof a couple times. Christine put the car in drive and headed north into Brownsville.